the MUTTS™
Autumn diaries

Other Books by Patrick McDonnell

Mutts
Cats and Dogs: Mutts II
More Shtuff: Mutts III
Yesh!: Mutts IV
Our Mutts: Five
A Little Look-See: Mutts VI
What Now: Mutts VII
I Want to Be the Kitty: Mutts VIII
Dog-Eared: Mutts IX
Who Let the Cat Out: Mutts X
Everyday Mutts
Animal Friendly
Call of the Wild
Stop and Smell the Roses
Earl & Mooch
Our Little Kat King
Bonk!
Cat Crazy
Living the Dream
The Mutts Diaries
Playtime
The Mutts Winter Diaries
ꞏꞏ
Mutts Sundays
Sunday Mornings
Sunday Afternoons
Sunday Evenings
Best of Mutts
ꞏꞏ
Shelter Stories
A Shtinky Little Christmas

the MUTTS™

Autumn diaries

• PATRICK McDONNELL •

Andrews McMeel
Publishing®

a division of Andrews McMeel Universal

WELL, EARL, NO MORE FUN AND GAMES — SHUMMER'S OVER.
BACK TO SHERIOUS BUSINESSH

Little Pink Sock
LITTLE PINK SOCK

?
MOOCH! WHERE ARE YOU GOING!?!
!!

PHILIPPE INVITED ME TO MIGRATE SOUTH WITH HIM.

PHILIPPE INVITED ME TO GO SOUTH WITH HIM.
SOUTH?
BUT YOU CAN'T FLY!?!
FLY?
I THOUGHT WE WERE TAKING A LIMO.

EARL
I'M GOING SOUTH WITH PHILIPPE
BUT MOOCH- HE MIGRATES 1,200 MILES!
1,200 MILES !?!
I SAID "SOUTH"— NOT "MARS"!

YUP, EARL, I'M GOING SOUTH WITH PHILIPPE AND HIS FLOCK!
AND WHERE ARE YOU GOING TO STAY WHEN YOU GET THERE !?!
WHICHEVER RESORT THEY BOOKED IS FINE WITH ME.

WHAT DID YOU PACK FOR YOUR TRIP SOUTH, MOOCH?
YOUR LUNCH.

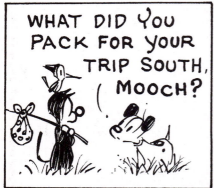

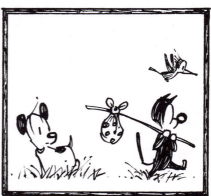

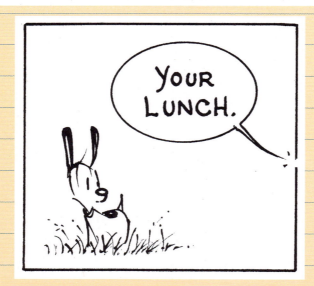

MOOCH
I THOUGHT YOU WERE MIGRATING SOUTH?
PHOOEY
THAT'S SHTRICTLY
FOR THE BIRDS.

WATCH THIS!
IT'S AUTUMN, BABY!

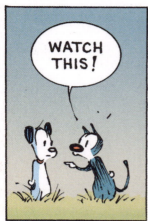

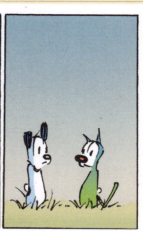

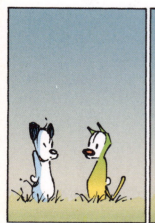

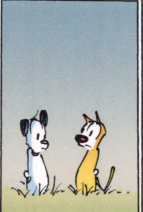

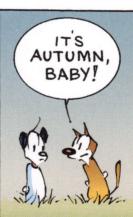

JULES!?!

I DIDN'T SEE THAT RAKE COMING.

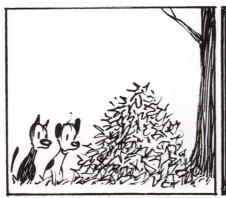

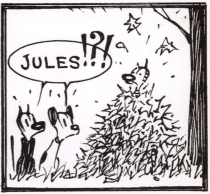

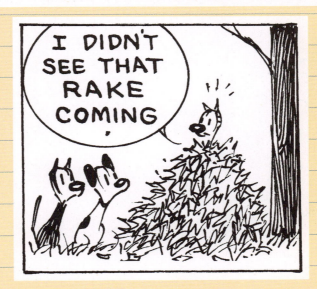

DON'T FORGET YOUR LUNCH AND LISTEN To YOUR TEACHER
MAKE US PROUD

MEOW!
...AND HE WOULDN'T BE BACK 'TIL THREE !!!

HOW DO YOU KNOW WHEN IT'S TIME TO FLY SOUTH?
A LITTLE VOICE TELLS ME.

C'MON, LET'S GO!
WE'RE LATE!
HURRY!

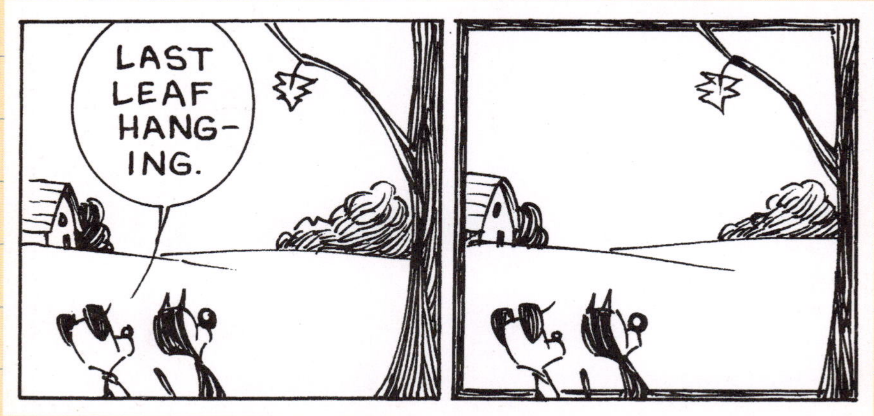
LAST LEAF HANG-ING.

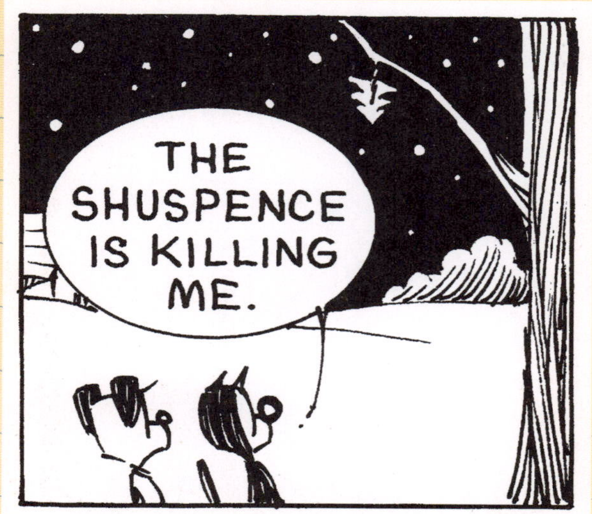
THE SHUSPENCE IS KILLING ME.

I'M WRITING THE BIRDS A POSTCARD.
DO YOU HAVE THEIR NEW ADDRESS?
YESH.

SOUTH.

BONK

NOW FOR THE EXTRA POINT!

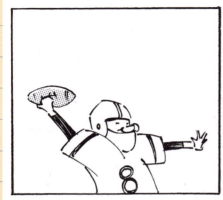

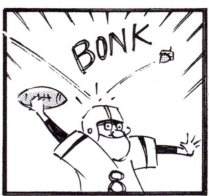

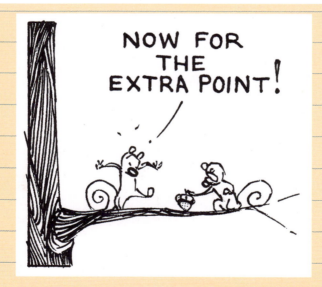

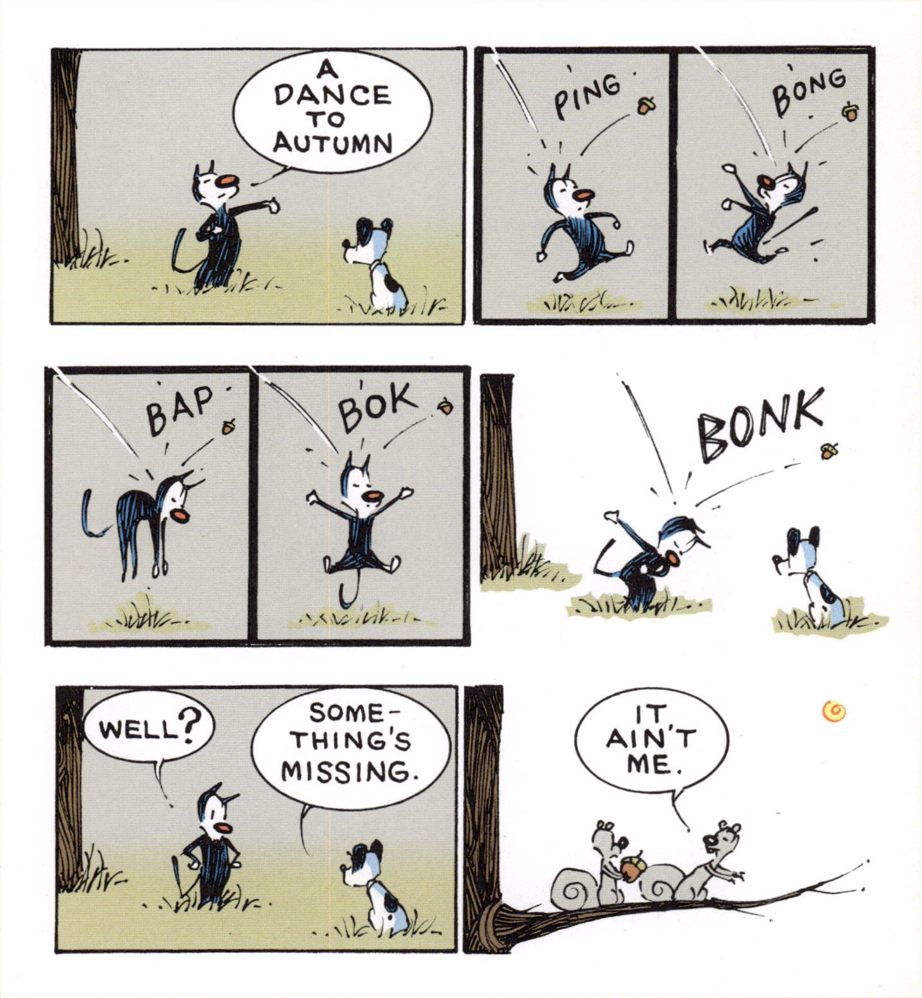
A DANCE TO AUTUMN
PING
BONG
BAP
BOK
BONK
WELL?
SOME-THING'S MISSING.
IT AIN'T ME.

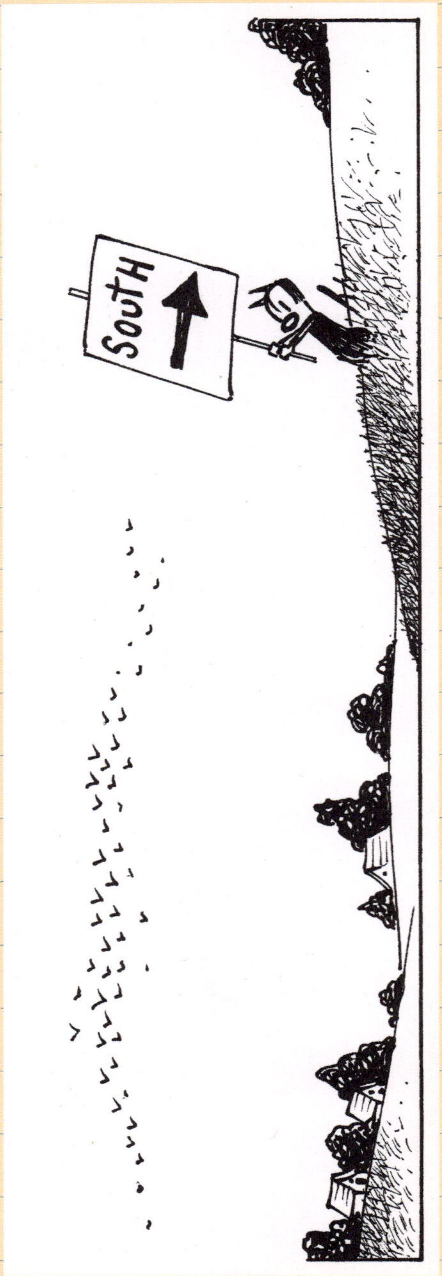
SOUTH

HEY, BIP, BOP- DID YOU MISS US?
BONK BONK
NOT IF I CAN HELP IT.

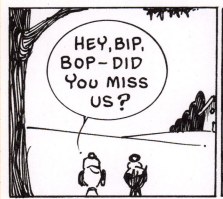

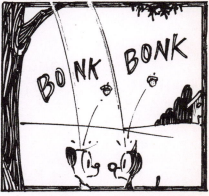

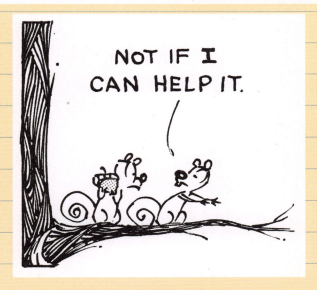

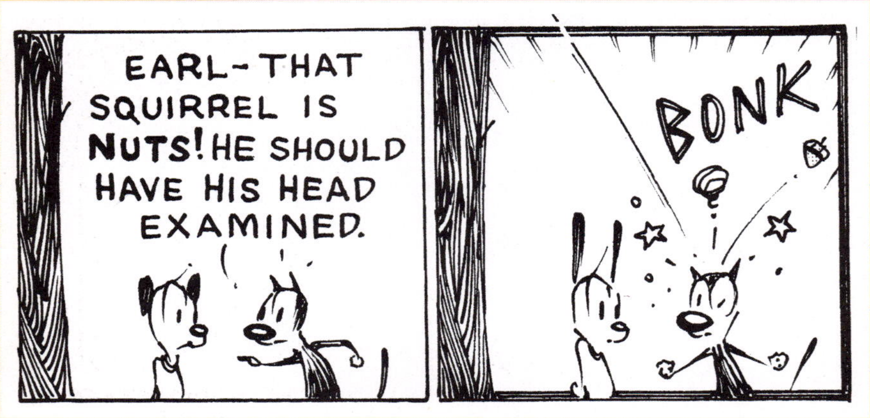
EARL- THAT SQUIRREL IS **NUTS!** HE SHOULD HAVE HIS HEAD EXAMINED.
BONK

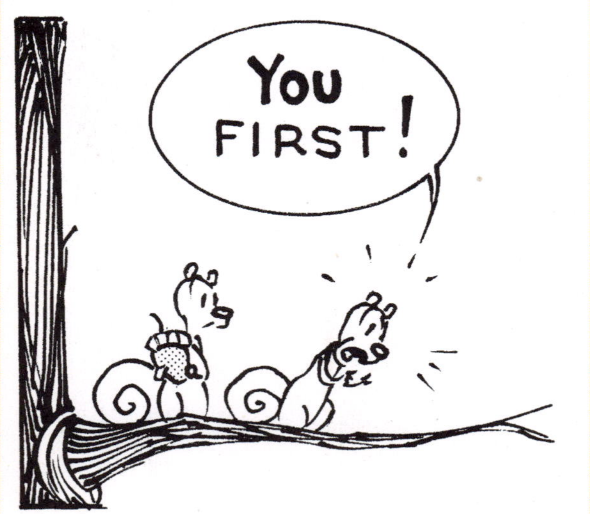
YOU FIRST!

LOOK OUT! THE WHOLE THING SHMIGHT BLOW!

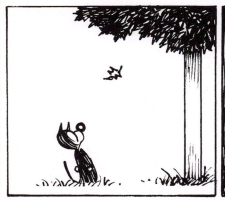

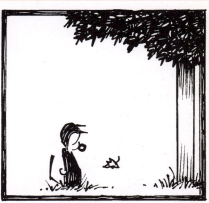

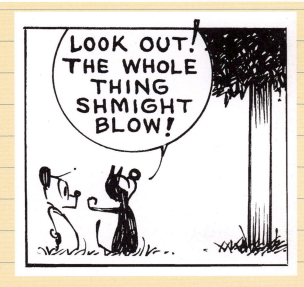

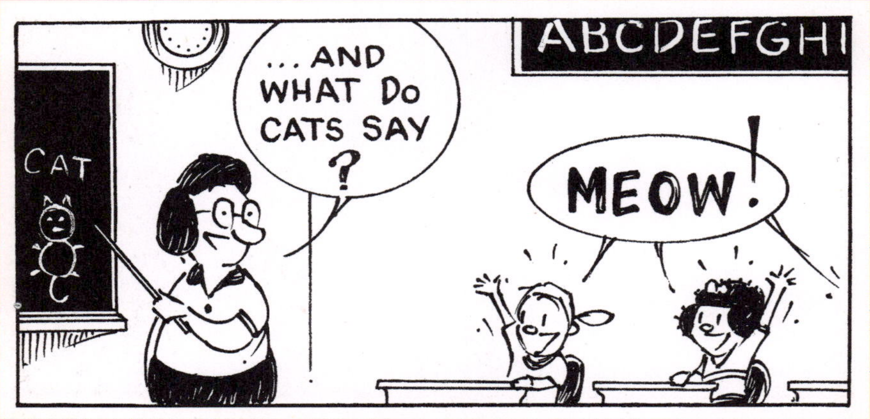
ABCDEFGHI
CAT
...AND WHAT DO CATS SAY?
MEOW!

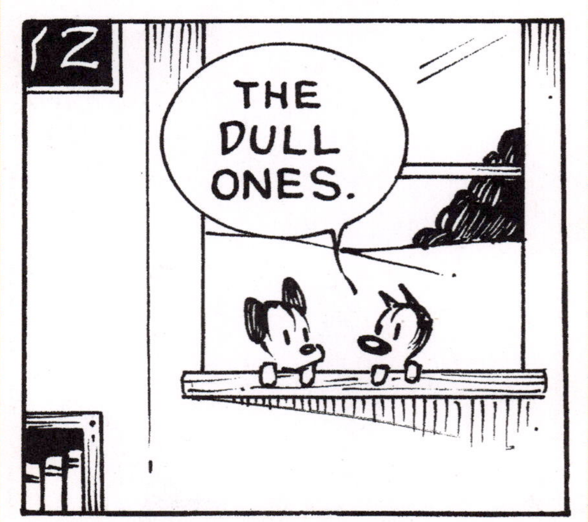
12
THE DULL ONES.

WHEN YOU GO SOUTH FOR THE WINTER- HOW DO YOU KNOW WHERE TO GO?
I HAVE A COMPASS IN MY HEAD.
WOW

IT MUST BE REALLY SHMALL.

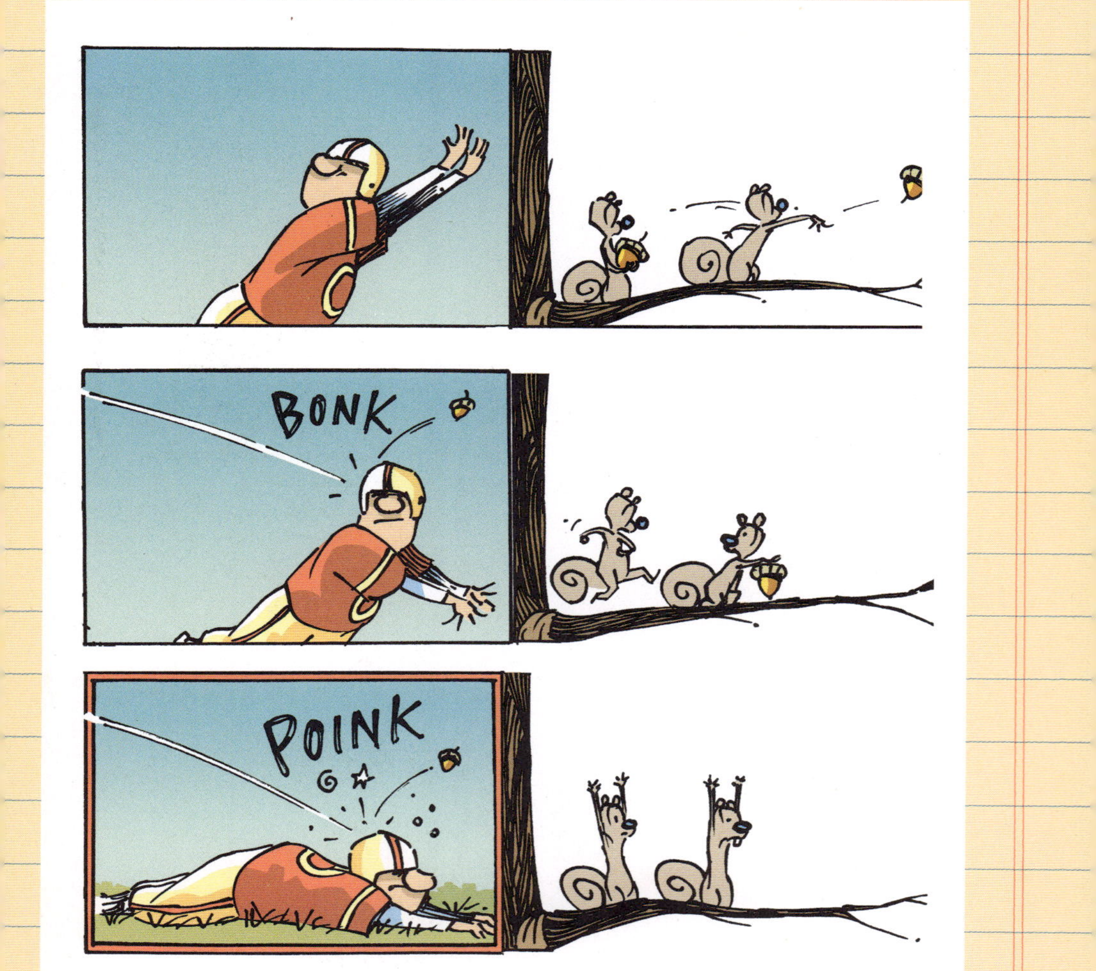
BONK
POINK

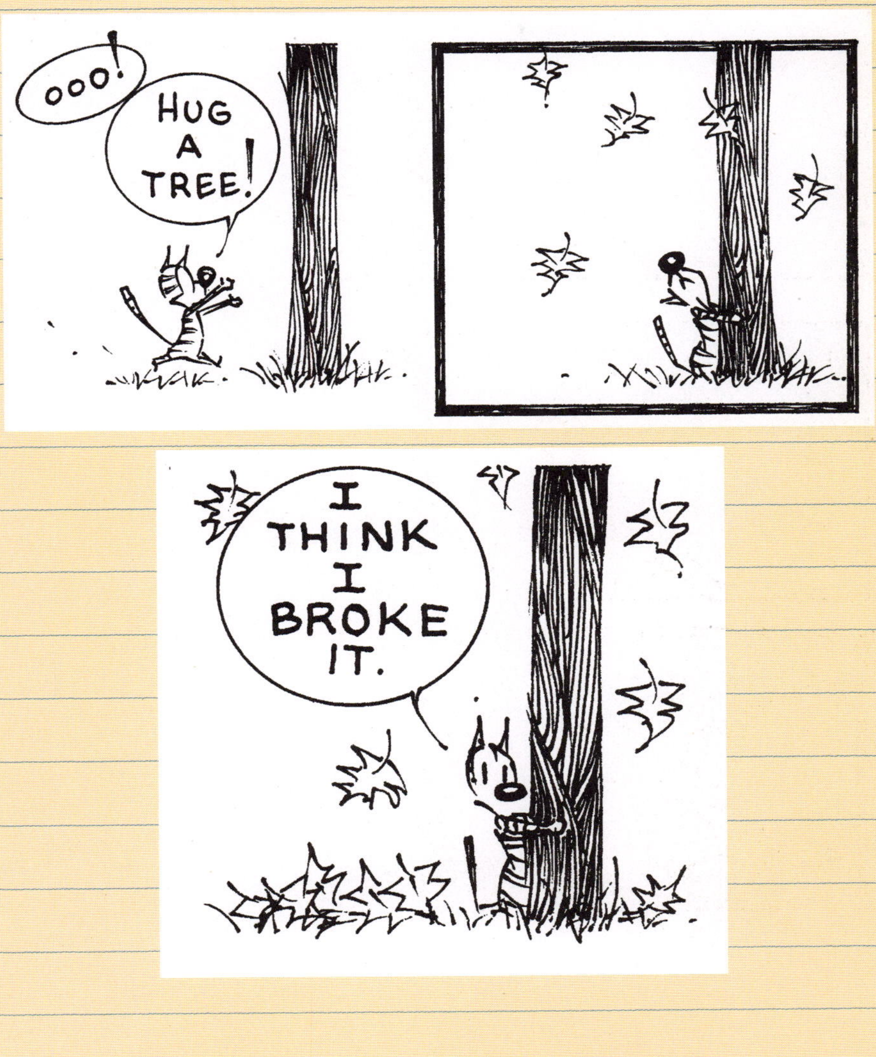
OOO!
HUG A TREE!
I THINK I BROKE IT.

BIP
BEEP
BONK
INSTANT MESSAGING.

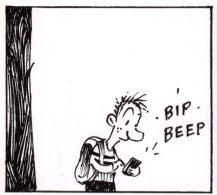

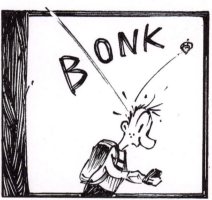

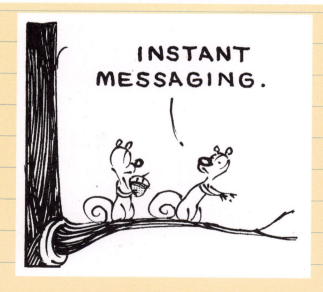

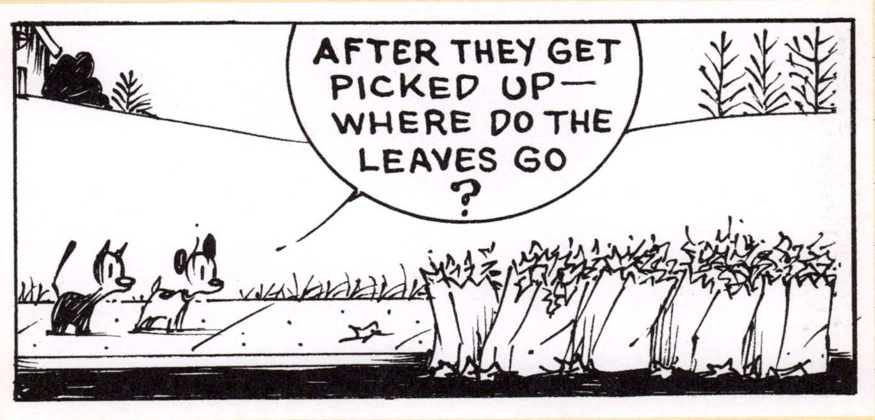
AFTER THEY GET PICKED UP— WHERE DO THE LEAVES GO ?

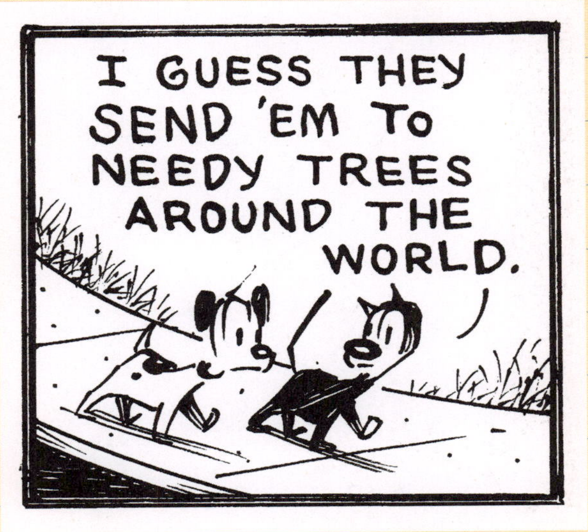
I GUESS THEY SEND 'EM TO NEEDY TREES AROUND THE WORLD.

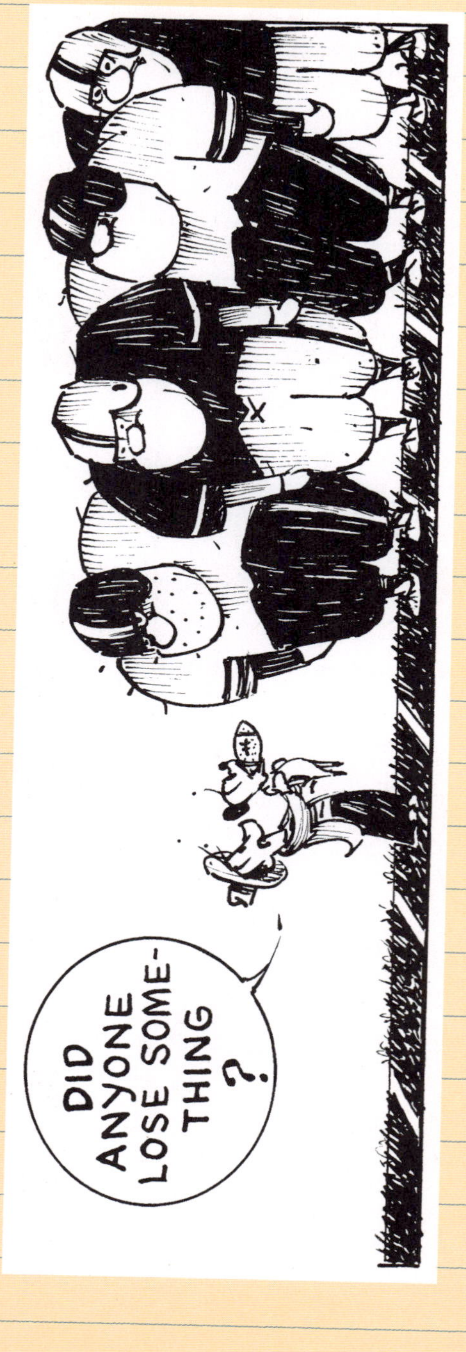
DID ANYONE LOSE SOME- THING ?

I'M GOING TO TRY CHANGING COLORS LIKE THE FALL LEAVES.
UMF
UGH
ARG!
STOP, MOOCH! YOU'RE TURNING BLUE!
YESH!

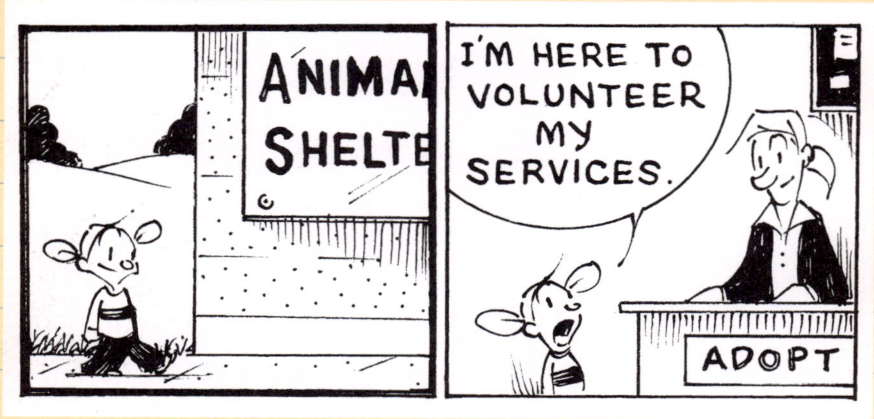
ANIMA
SHELTE
I'M HERE TO VOLUNTEER MY SERVICES.
ADOPT

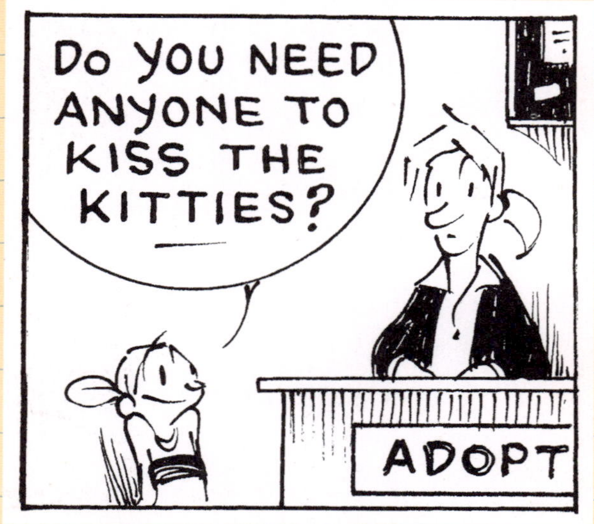
DO YOU NEED ANYONE TO KISS THE KITTIES?
ADOPT

SHELTERS ARE ALWAYS LOOKING FOR **ALL** TYPES
ADOPT
OF VOLUNTEER SERVICES.
ADOPT
COULD YOU USE AN EXPERIENCED BELLY-RUBBER?
ADOPT

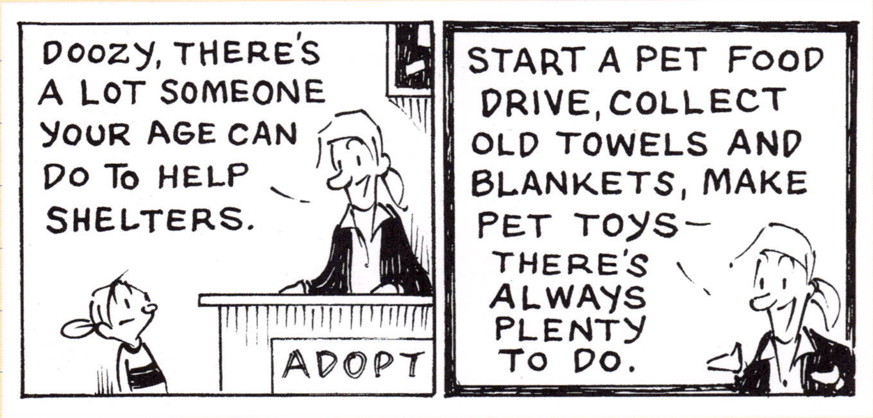
DOOZY, THERE'S A LOT SOMEONE YOUR AGE CAN DO TO HELP SHELTERS.
ADOPT
START A PET FOOD DRIVE, COLLECT OLD TOWELS AND BLANKETS, MAKE PET TOYS—
THERE'S ALWAYS PLENTY TO DO.

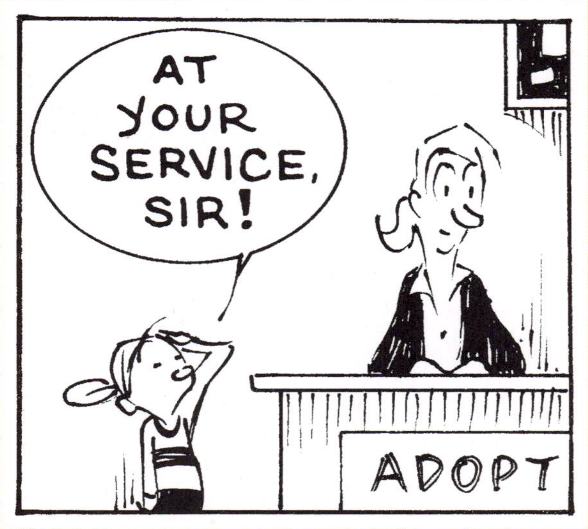
AT YOUR SERVICE, SIR!
ADOPT

ANIM
SHELT
WHAT'S DOOZY DOING?
SHE'S SERV-ING.
IS IT DINNER ALREADY?

"No joy can equal the joy of serving others."
—Sai Baba

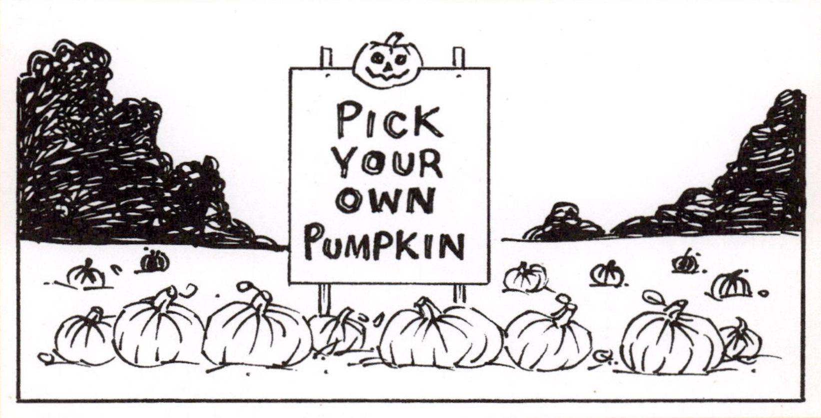
PICK
YOUR
OWN
PUMPKIN

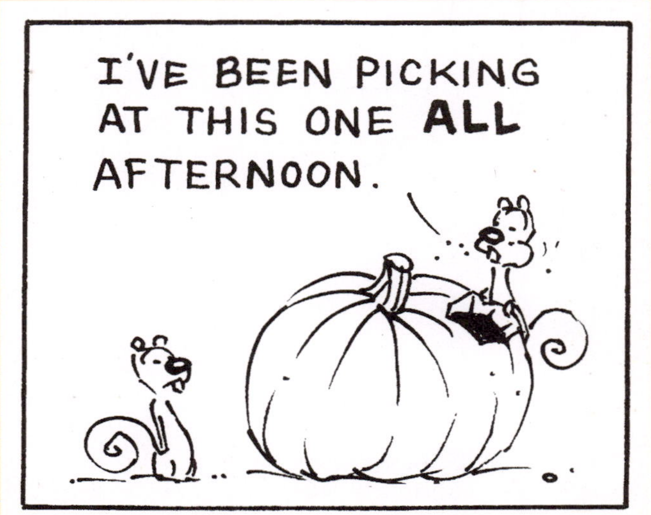
I'VE BEEN PICKING AT THIS ONE **ALL** AFTERNOON.

AHH, SHNELLY-
ONCE AGAIN
IT'S TIME FOR
THE LEAVES
TO FALL.
AMONG
OTHER
THINGS

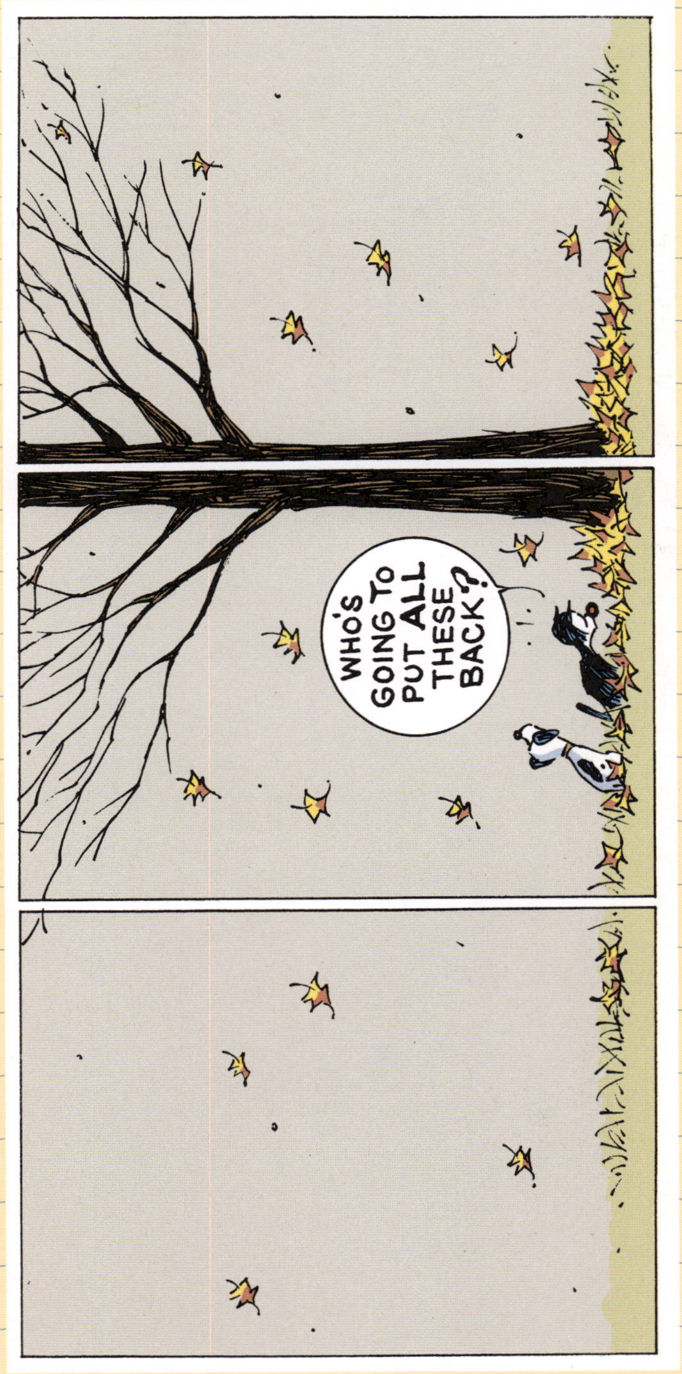
WHO'S GOING TO PUT ALL THESE BACK?

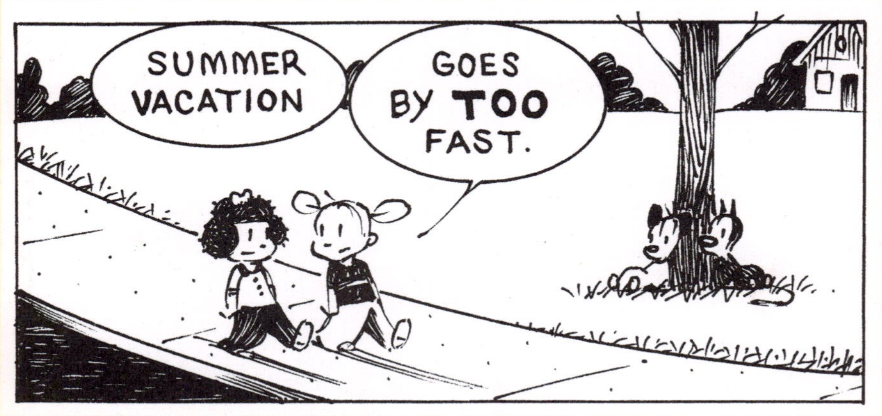
SUMMER VACATION
GOES BY TOO FAST.

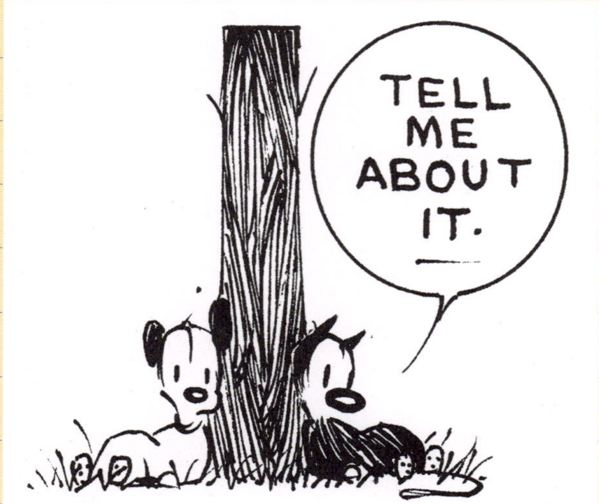
TELL ME ABOUT IT.

MOOCH, ARE YOU AFRAID OF – PUMPKINS?
FOO! WHY SHOULD I BE SHCARED OF PUMPKINS!?!
WHY NOT?

PUMPKINS CAN'T TALK!!!
I BEG TO DIFFER.
UGH.
SHOME FOODS DISHAGREE WITH ME.

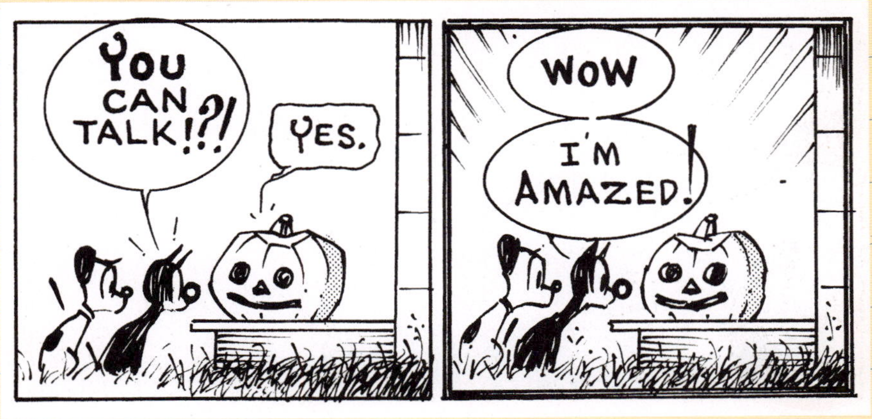
YOU CAN TALK!?!
YES.
WOW
I'M AMAZED!

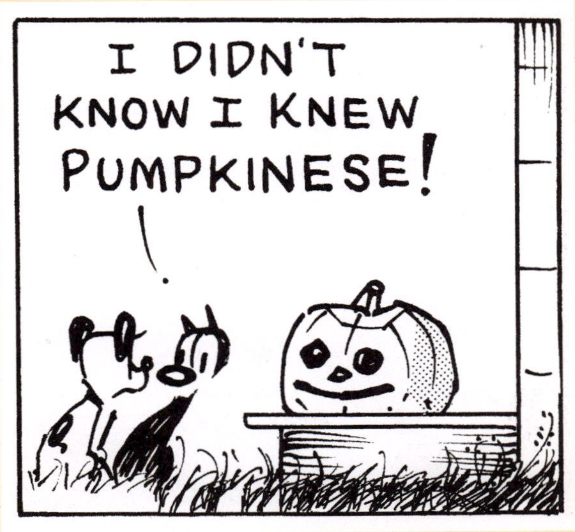
I DIDN'T KNOW I KNEW PUMPKINESE!

EVEN IF PUMPKINS COULD TALK- SHO WHAT!?!
HE'D PROBABLY JUST SAY SHOMETHING SHTUPID, RIGHT?

YESH.

SO- WHAT'S A PUMPKIN'S PHILOSOPHY?
LIFE IS GOURD.

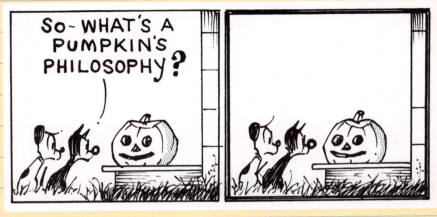

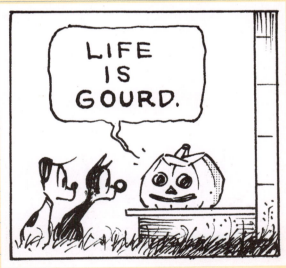

A TALKING PUMPKIN!?! NOW I'VE SHEEN EVERYTHING!
HA!
NOT EVERY-THING.

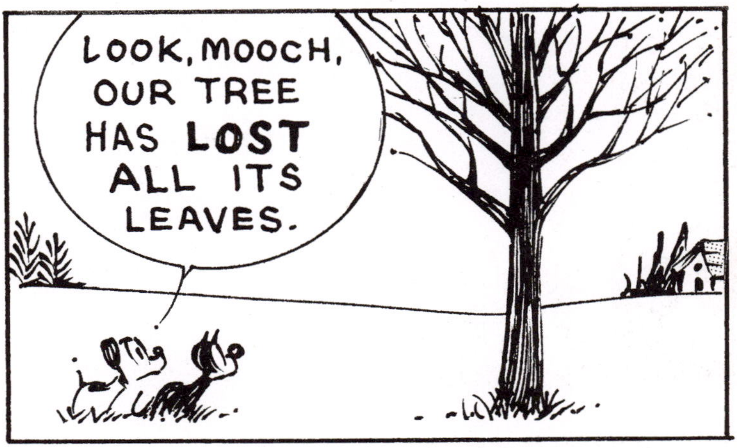
LOOK, MOOCH, OUR TREE HAS **LOST** ALL ITS LEAVES.

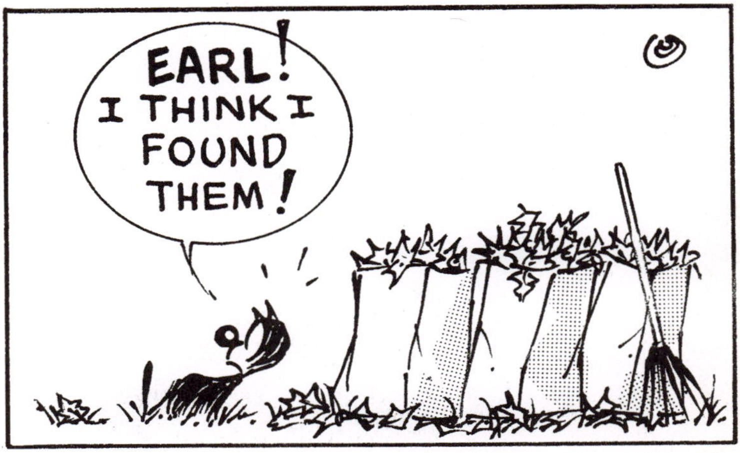
EARL! I THINK I FOUND THEM!

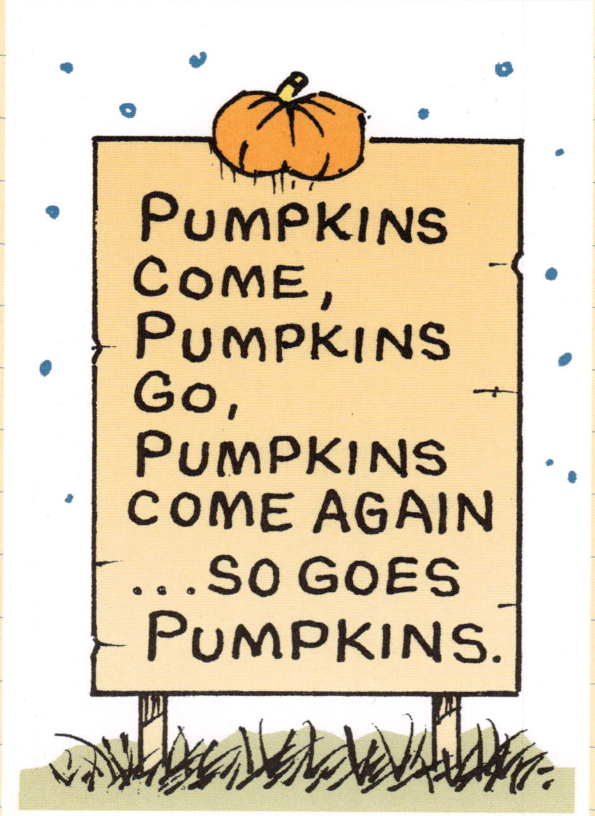
PUMPKINS COME, PUMPKINS GO, PUMPKINS COME AGAIN . . . SO GOES PUMPKINS.

PICK YOUR OWN PUMPKIN
I CHOOSE NOT TO CHOOSE!
GNAW
I CHEWS TO CHOOSE!

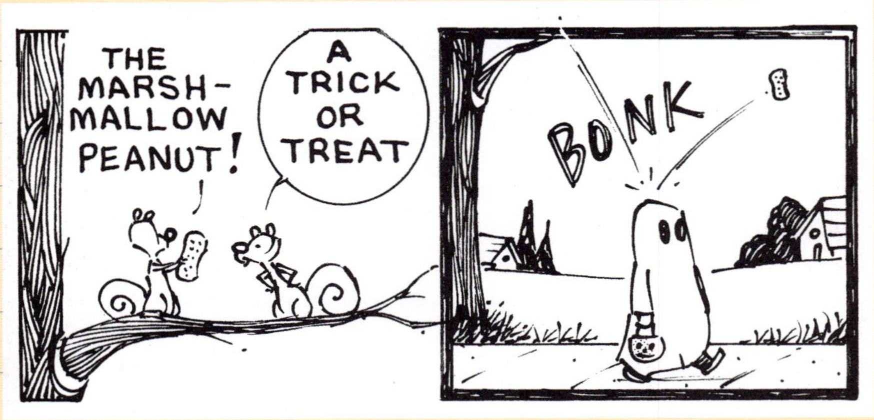
THE MARSH-MALLOW PEANUT!
A TRICK OR TREAT
BONK

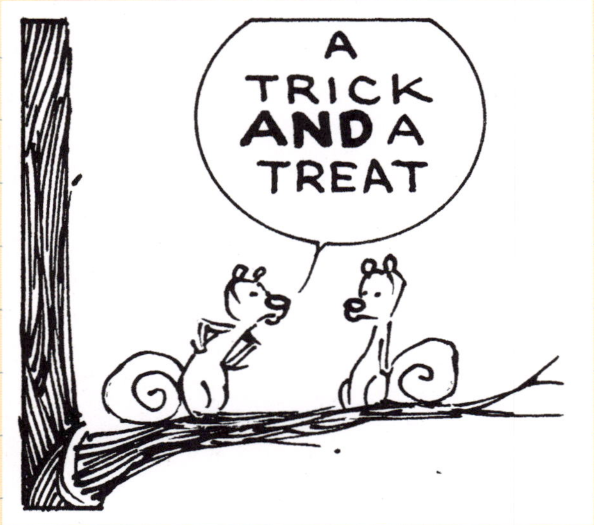
A TRICK **AND** A TREAT

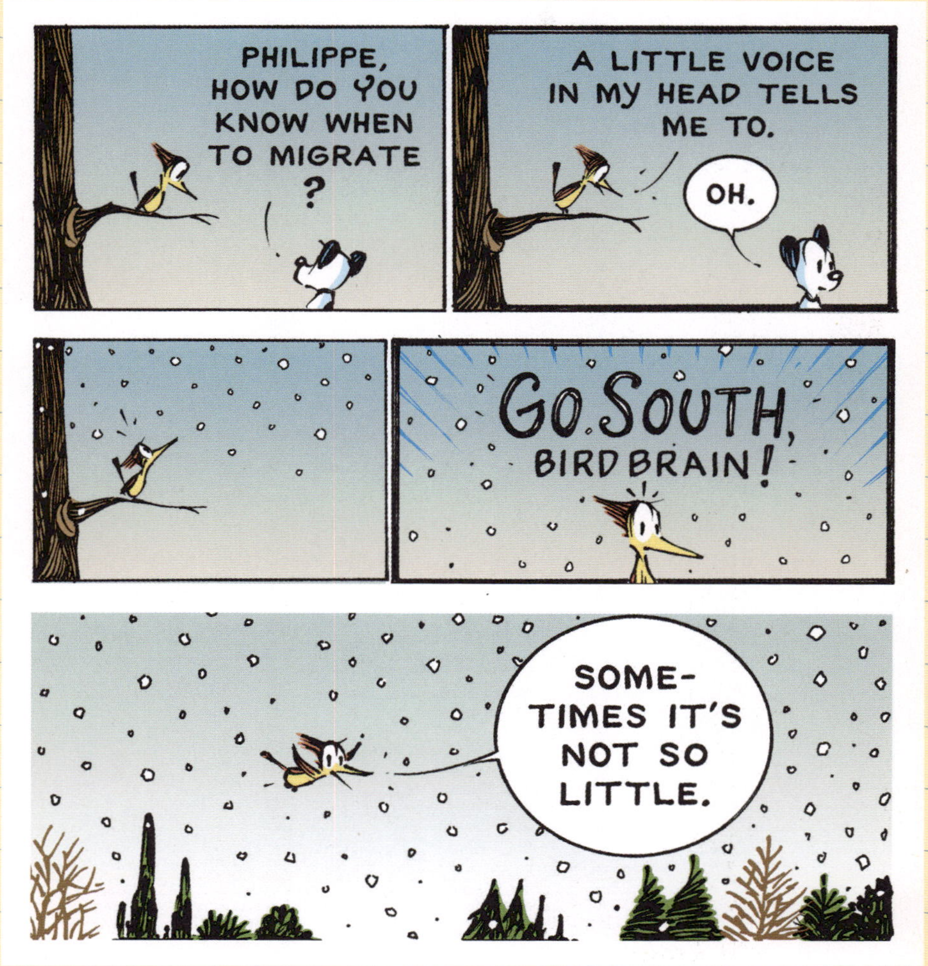
PHILIPPE, HOW DO YOU KNOW WHEN TO MIGRATE ?
A LITTLE VOICE IN MY HEAD TELLS ME TO.
OH.
GO SOUTH, BIRD BRAIN!
SOME-TIMES IT'S NOT SO LITTLE.

YOU FORGOT YOUR PANTS.

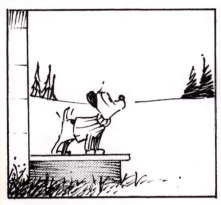

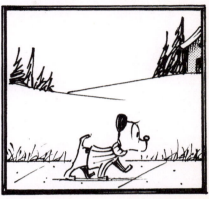

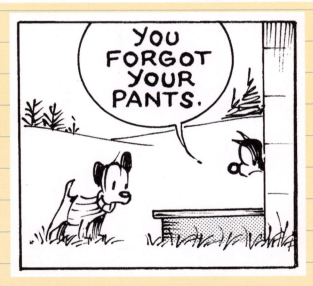

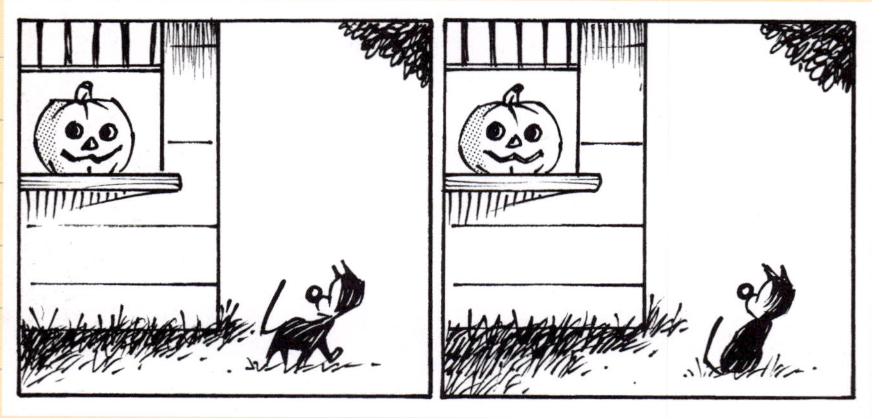

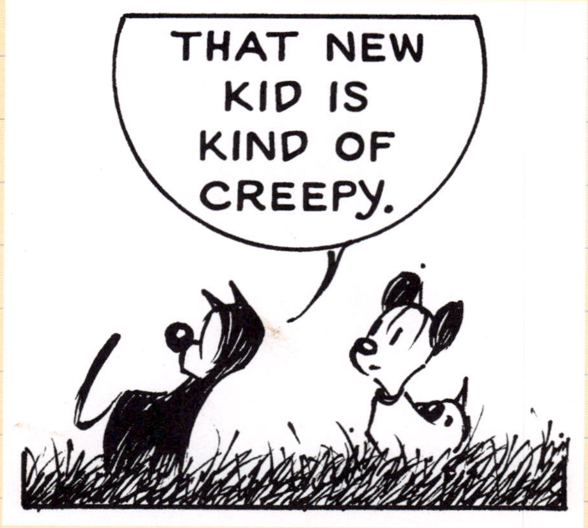
THAT NEW KID IS KIND OF CREEPY.

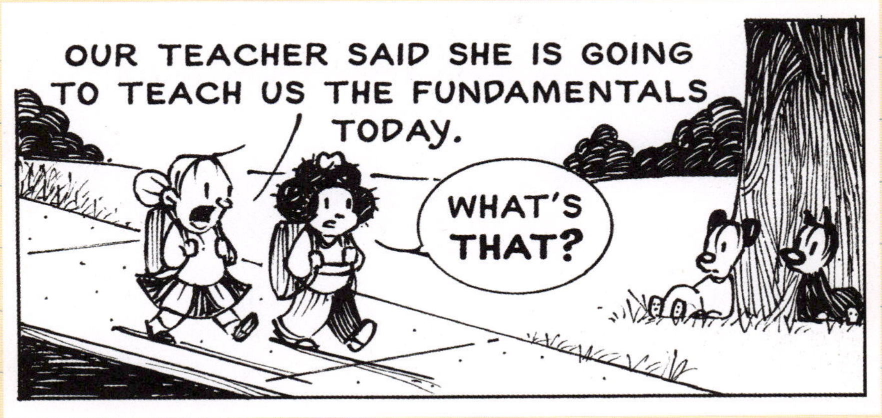
OUR TEACHER SAID SHE IS GOING TO TEACH US THE FUNDAMENTALS TODAY.
WHAT'S THAT?

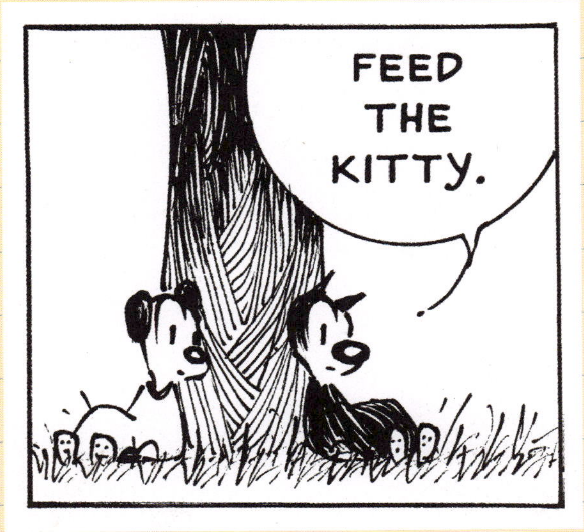
FEED THE KITTY.

A POEM FOR PUMPKINS
PUMPKINS COME, PUMPKINS GO, PUMPKINS COME AGAIN. SO GOES PUMPKINS.

I WISH I HAD A TOMATO.

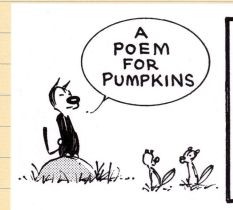

SHELTER STORIES
"RILEY"
A NEW HOME
A NEW START
A NEW LIFE

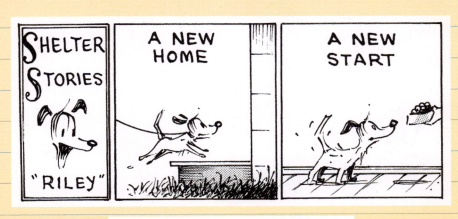

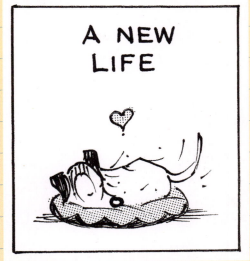

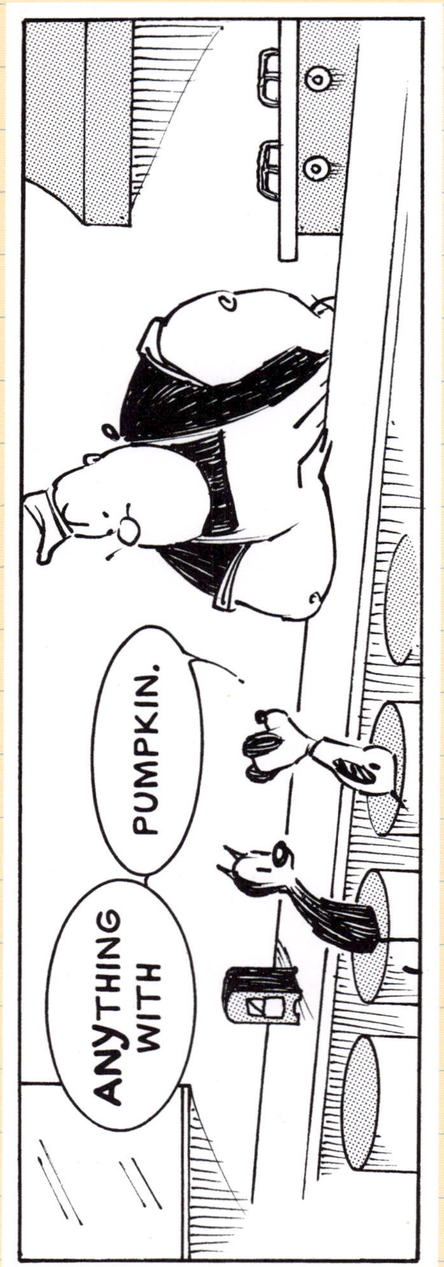
ANYTHING WITH
PUMPKIN.

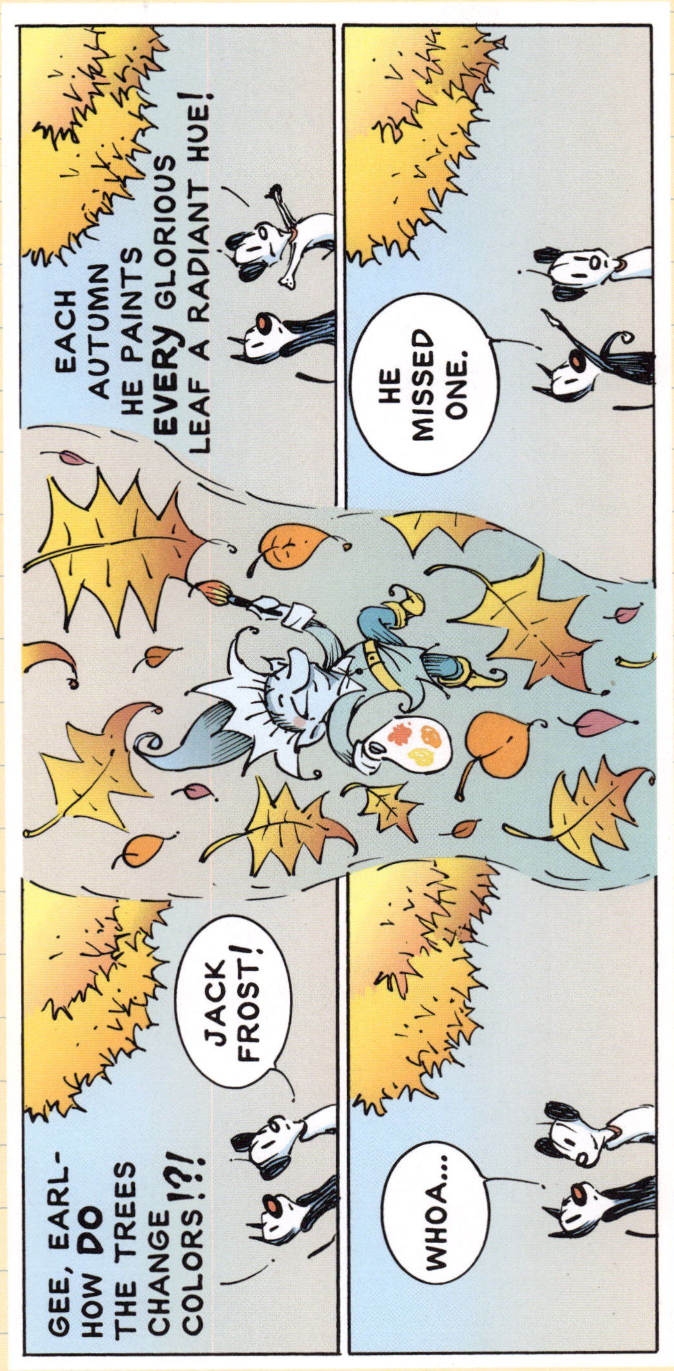
GEE, EARL- HOW DO THE TREES CHANGE COLORS!?!
JACK FROST!
EACH AUTUMN HE PAINTS EVERY GLORIOUS LEAF A RADIANT HUE!
WHOA...
HE MISSED ONE.

MY OZZIE'S CARVING A PUMPKIN
YESH!
WOW!
IT LOOKS JUST LIKE ONE!

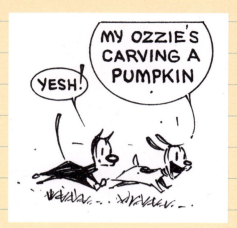

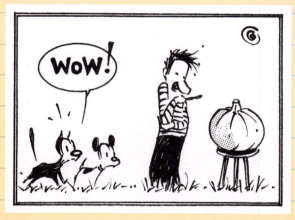

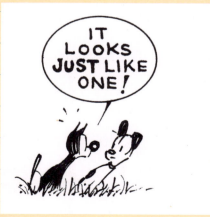

SIGH
WHAT'S WRONG, EARL?
ALL THE BIRDS HAVE GONE SOUTH, MOOCH
AND I MISS THEM SO.
SIGH

WHAT'S IT LIKE OUT, EARL?
PRETTY WINDY.

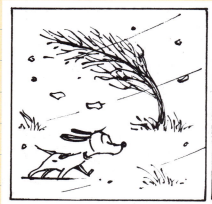

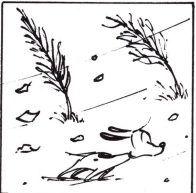

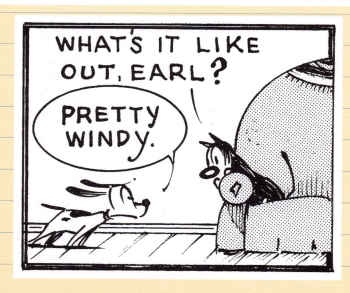

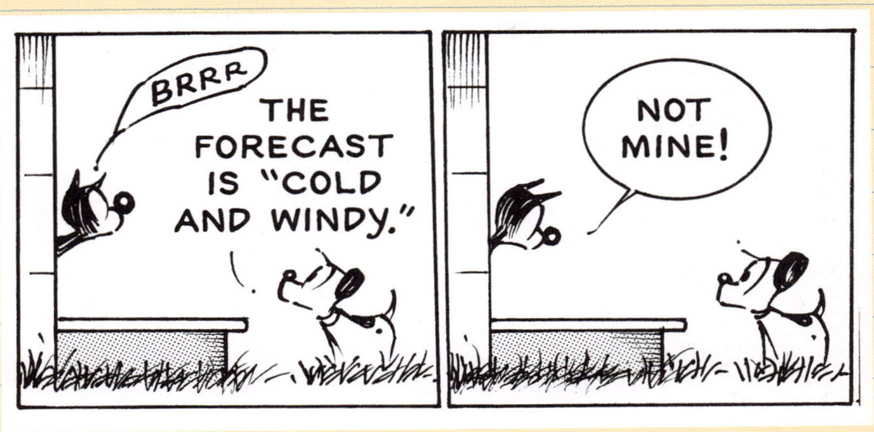
BRRR
THE FORECAST IS "COLD AND WINDY."
NOT MINE!

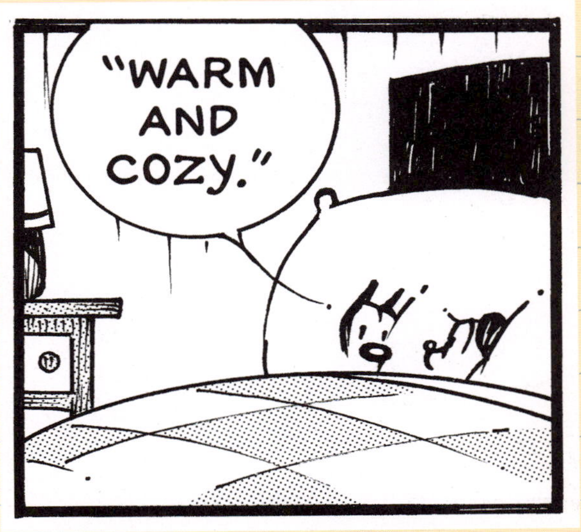
"WARM AND COZY."

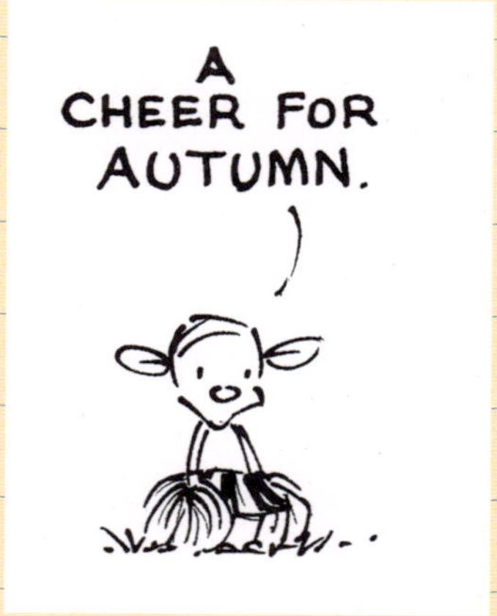
A CHEER FOR AUTUMN.

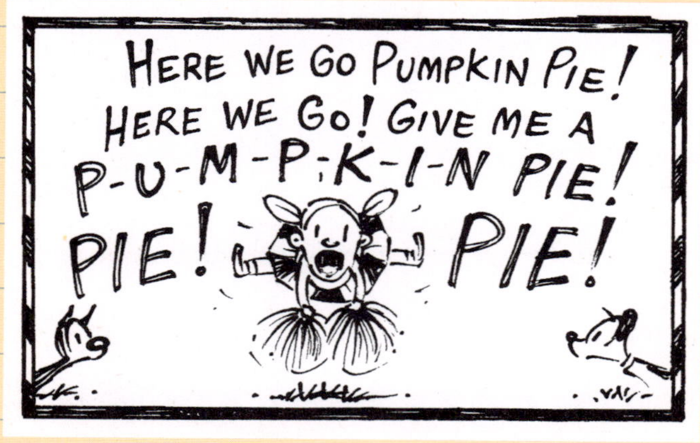
HERE WE GO PUMPKIN PIE! HERE WE GO! GIVE ME A P-U-M-P-K-I-N PIE!
PIE!
PIE!

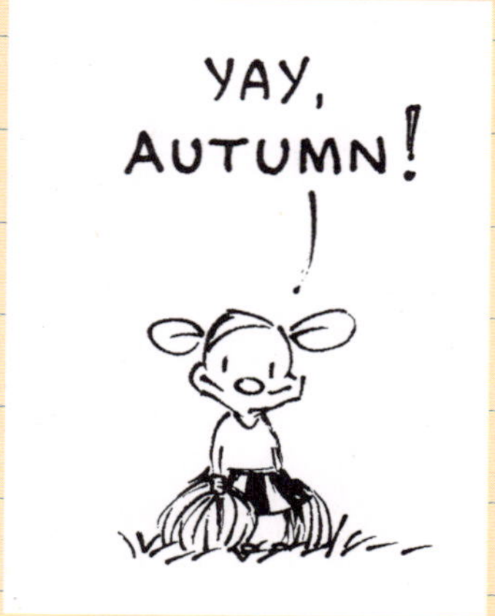
YAY, AUTUMN!

SHELTER STORIES UPDATE

"FLOP"

SIX YEARS AGO I TOLD EVERY-ONE COMING TO THE SHELTER TO "THINK BUNNY"

BUNNY. BUNNY! BUNNY!

IT WORKED.

SHELTER **S**TORIES

"REGGIE"

WOW! I'VE BEEN ADOPTED!

MY NEW FAMILY HAS A NICE LITTLE HOUSE AND A SWEET SMALL YARD—

AND REALLY **BIG** HEARTS!

ARF.

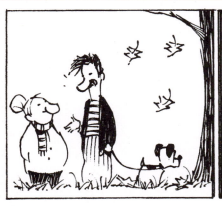

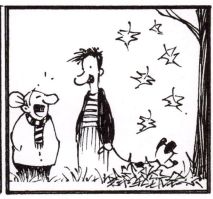

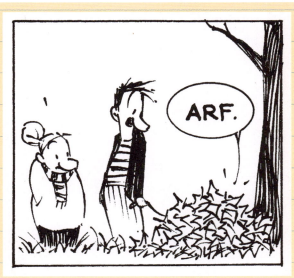

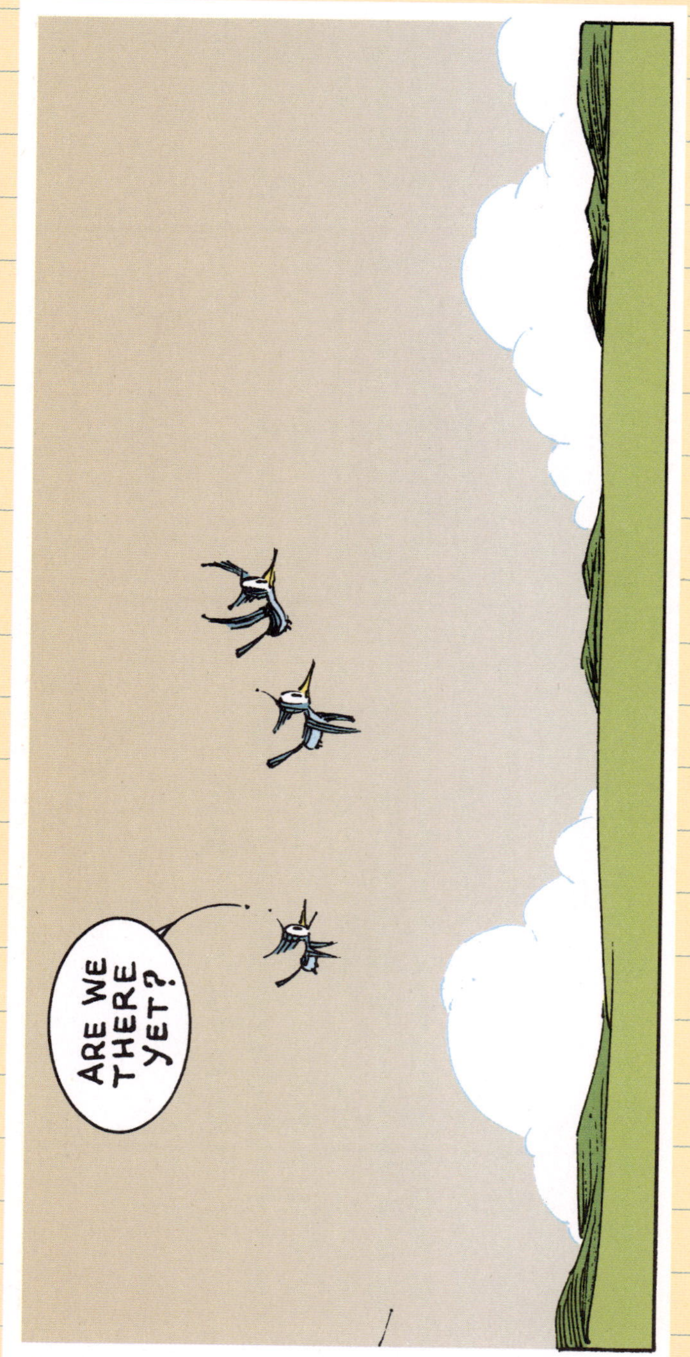
ARE WE THERE YET?

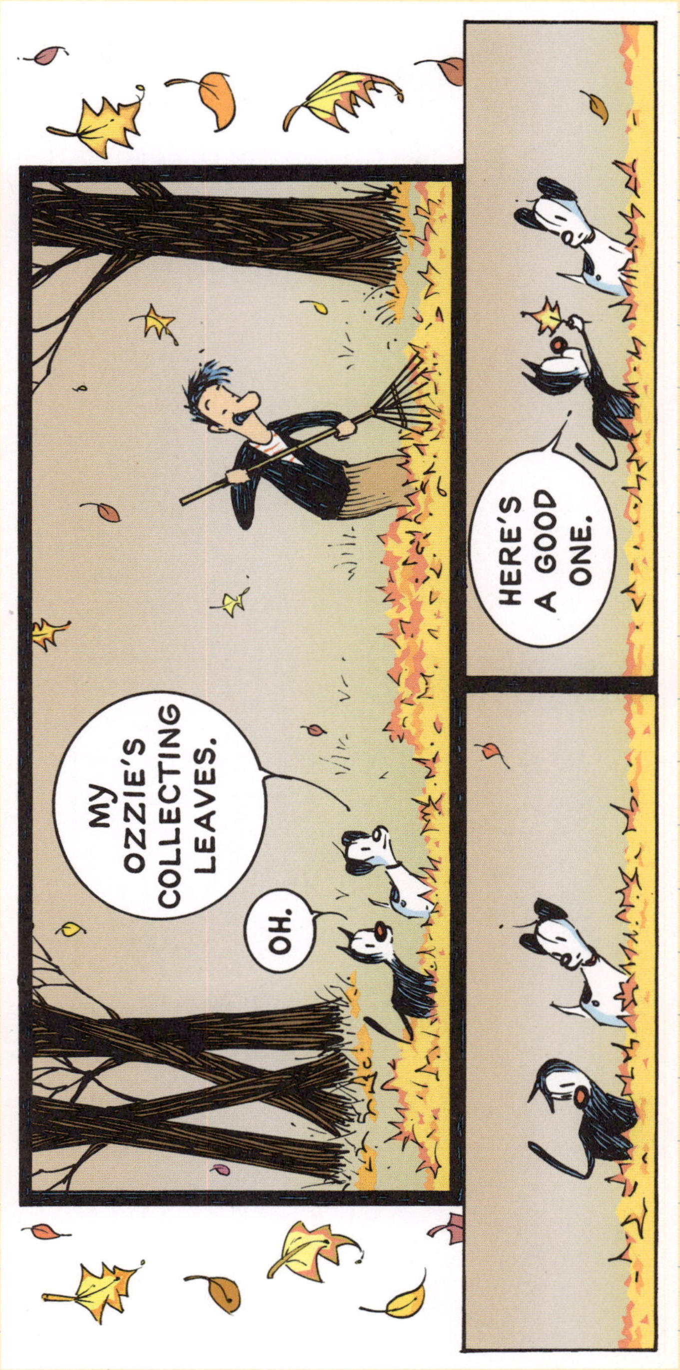

MY OZZIE'S COLLECTING LEAVES.
OH.
HERE'S A GOOD ONE.

LET IT GO.

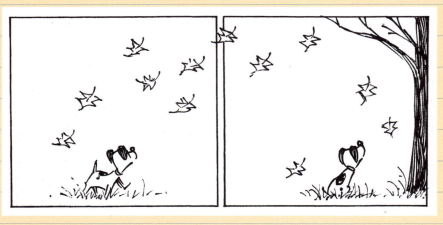

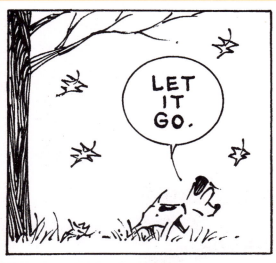

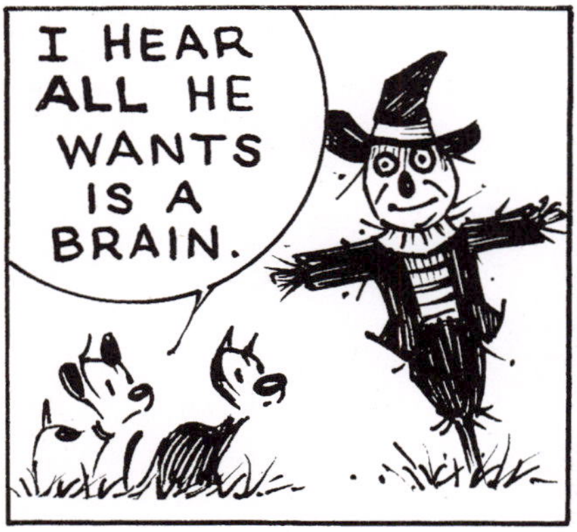
I HEAR ALL HE WANTS IS A BRAIN.

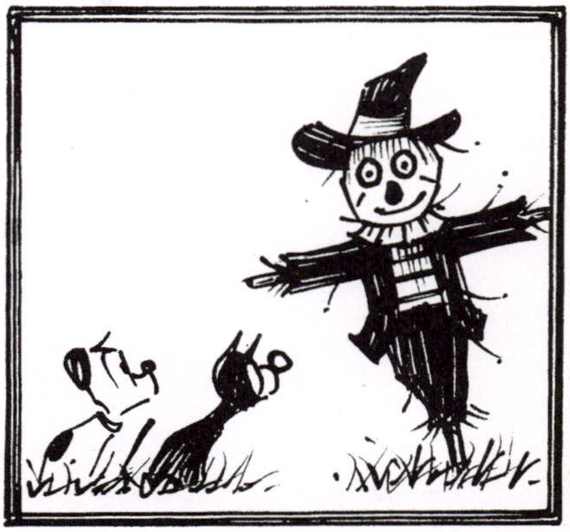

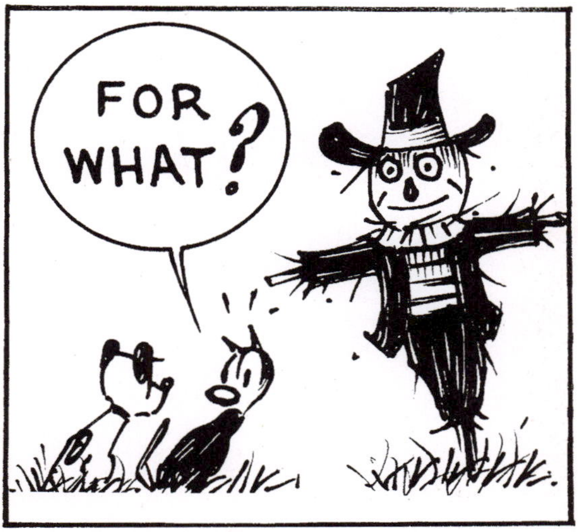
FOR WHAT?

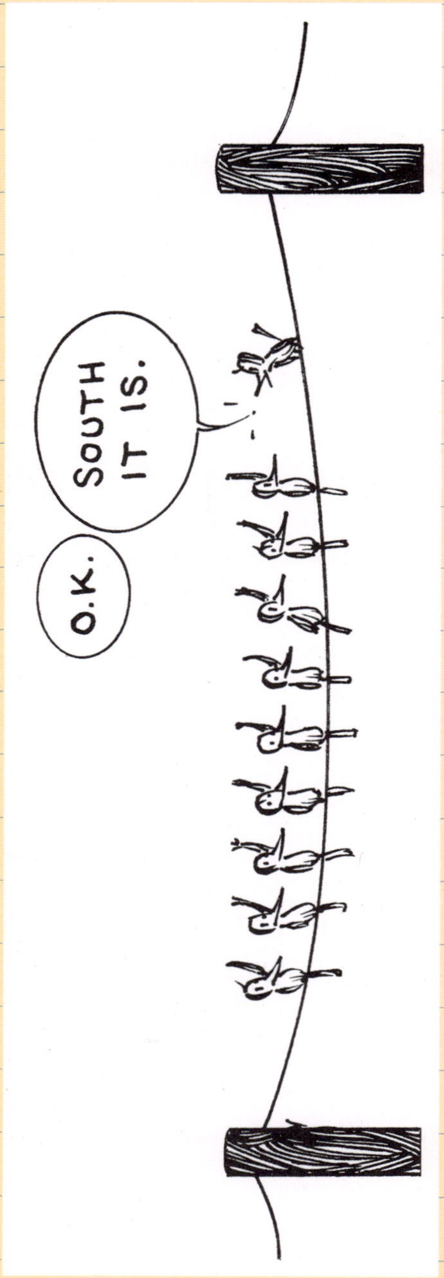
O.K.
SOUTH IT IS.

IT'S OFFICIALLY AUTUMN, MOOCH.
YESH.
LET THE PUMPKIN PIES BEGIN!

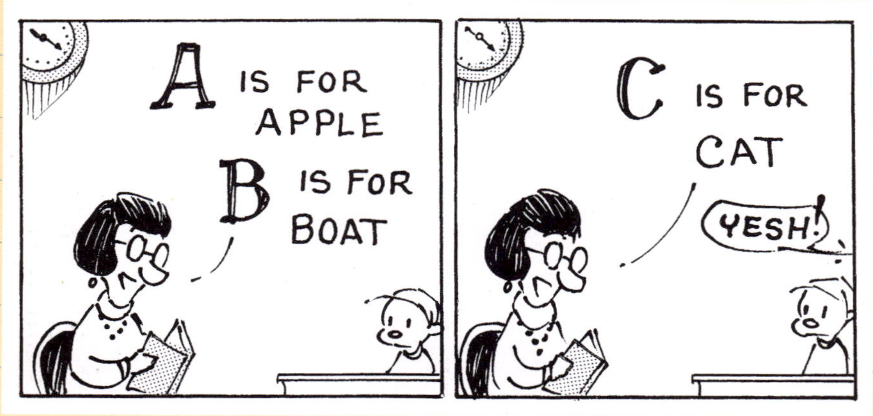
A IS FOR APPLE
B IS FOR BOAT
C IS FOR CAT
YESH!

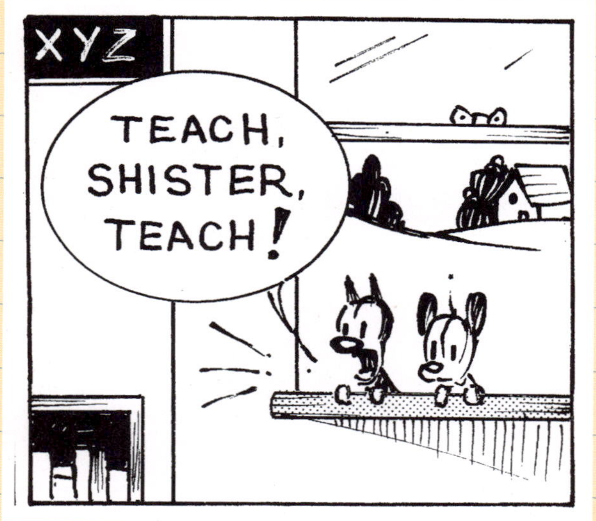
XYZ
TEACH, SHISTER, TEACH!

F IS FOR FOOT
G IS FOR GOAT
H IS FOR HOUSE
OOF!

YZ
THIS SHTORY DOESN'T HAVE MUCH OF A PLOT.

V
W
X
Y

Z

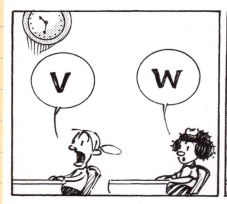

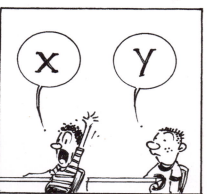

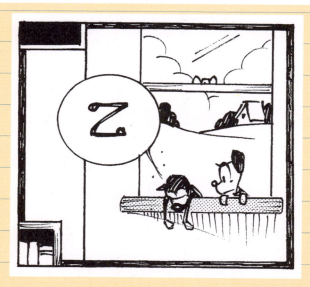

BOYS, IT'S TIME TO GO SOUTH! I **FEEL** IT IN MY BONES!
LET ME TRY!
MY BONES ARE HAPPY HERE.

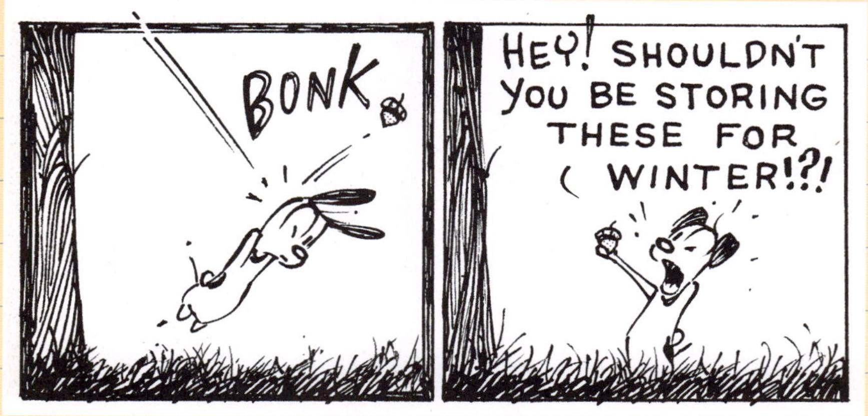
BONK
HEY! SHOULDN'T YOU BE STORING THESE FOR WINTER!?!

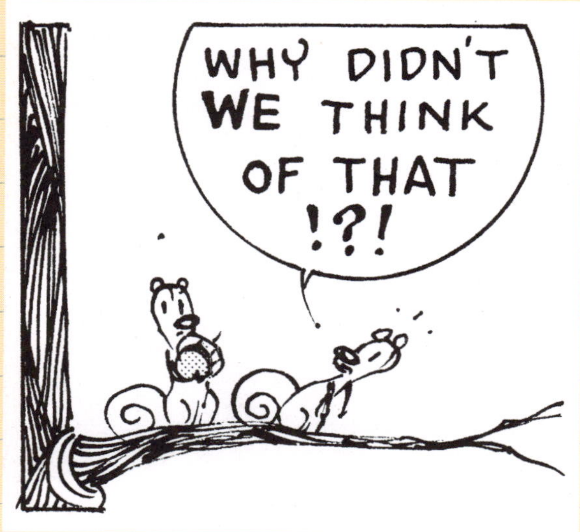
WHY DIDN'T WE THINK OF THAT !?!

IT'S OFFICIALLY AUTUMN, MOOCH.
THAT FIGURES
THIS MORNING
I FELT LIKE BOBBING FOR APPLES.

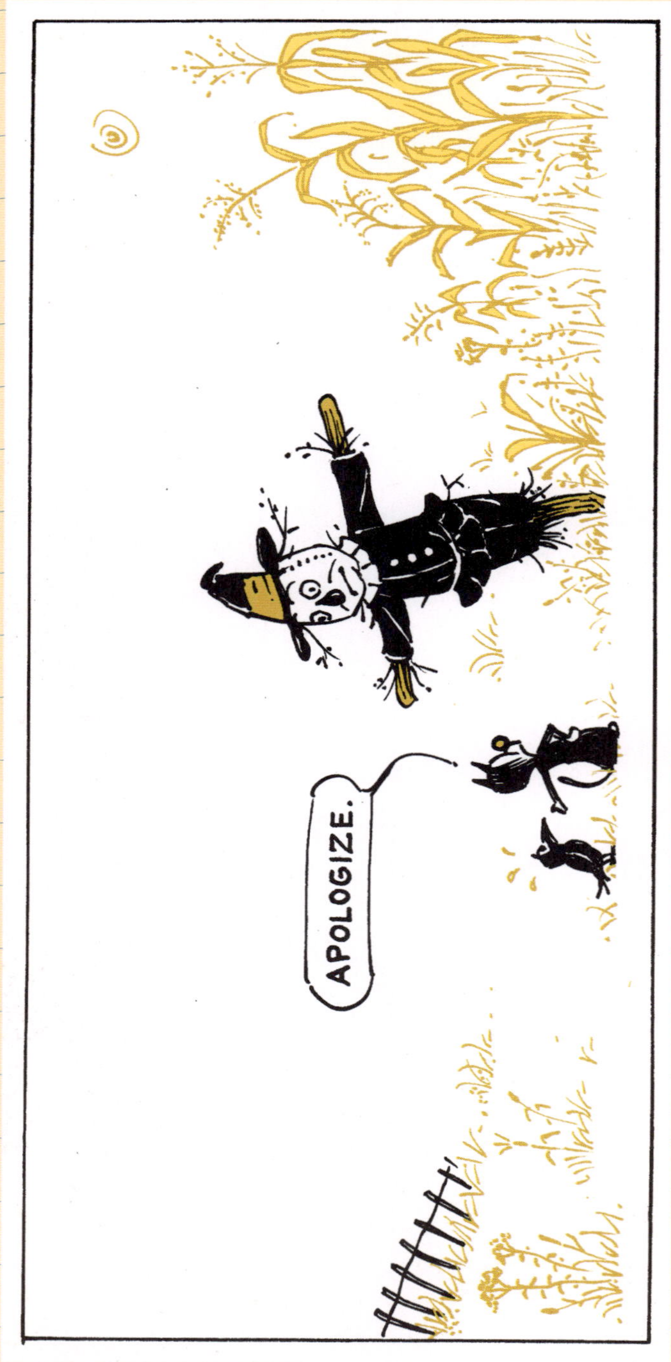
APOLOGIZE.

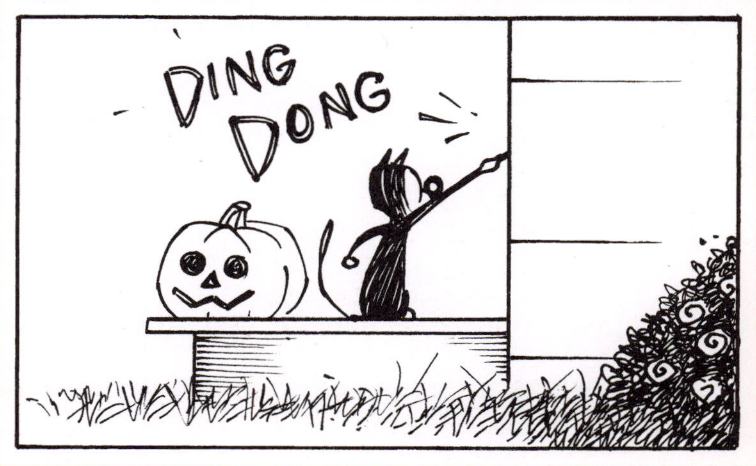
DING
DONG

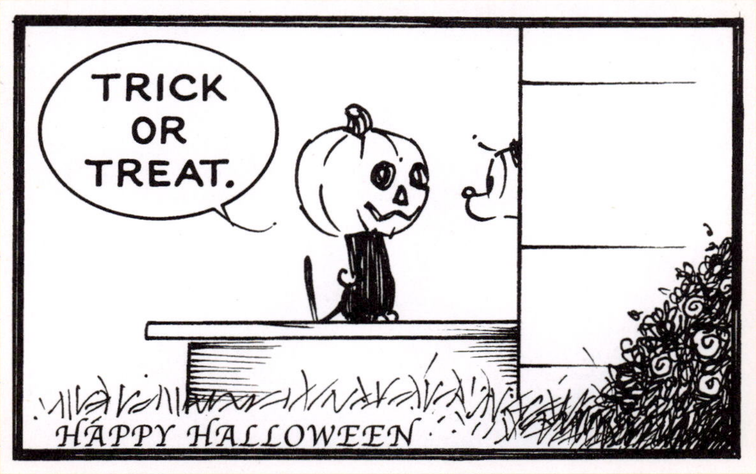
TRICK OR TREAT.
HAPPY HALLOWEEN

POOF! I'M "PROSHPERO" THE CAT WIZARD!
?!
AND WHAT MAKES YOU A WIZARD!?!
THE HAT FOR SHTARTS.

A SILLY HAT DOES NOT MAKE YOU A WIZARD!!!
OF COURSHE NOT.
THE WAND DOES.

A SILLY HAT AND A CAT TOY WAND DOES **NOT** MAKE YOU A WIZARD!
YESH! THAT'S WHY I HAVE MY MAGIC BOOK OF SHPELLS!
A DICTION-ARY !?!
WITH THIS I CAN **SHPELL** ANYTHING!!!

I, "PROSHPERO"- CAT WIZARD, CAN READ **MINDS**!
MMMMMM... YOU'RE THINKING I **CAN'T** DO IT.
WOW. YOU'RE GOOD.
I **KNEW** THAT.

"PROSHPERO" LOVES THIS TIME OF YEAR– THERE'S MAGIC IN THE AIR!
BONK

NOW YOU SEE IT– NOW YOU DON'T.

I, "PROSHPERO"-THE GREAT CAT WIZARD, WILL NOW DISH-APPEAR!
POOF!
DID I FORGET SHOME-THING?

WATCH 'MOJO,' MY SHORCERER'S APPRENTICE, CAST A SHPELL!
IPPIDY · BIPPIDY BZZSH · BZZSH BZZZ · FWEEE
POO!

A 'SPELLING' BEE!?!
YESH.
BZZZ

PROSHPERO, CAN YOU MAKE A PUMPKIN DISAPPEAR?
SURE... CLOSE YOUR EYES.
POOF!
IT'S STILL HERE.
I SAID- 'CLOSE YOUR EYES'

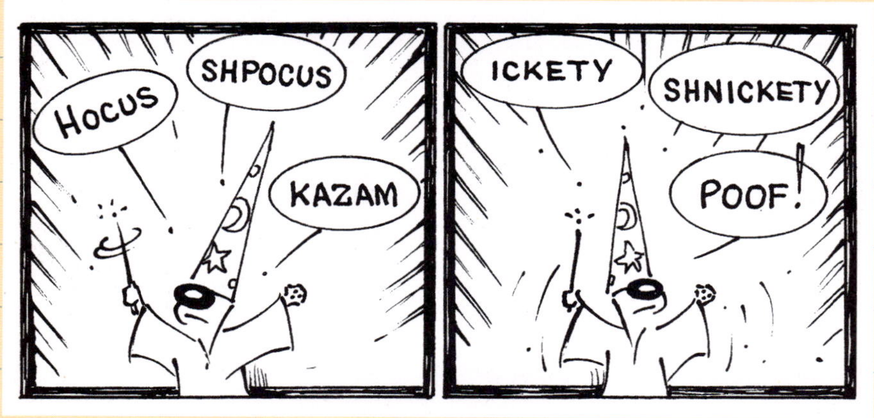
HOCUS
SHPOCUS
KAZAM
ICKETY
SHNICKETY
POOF!

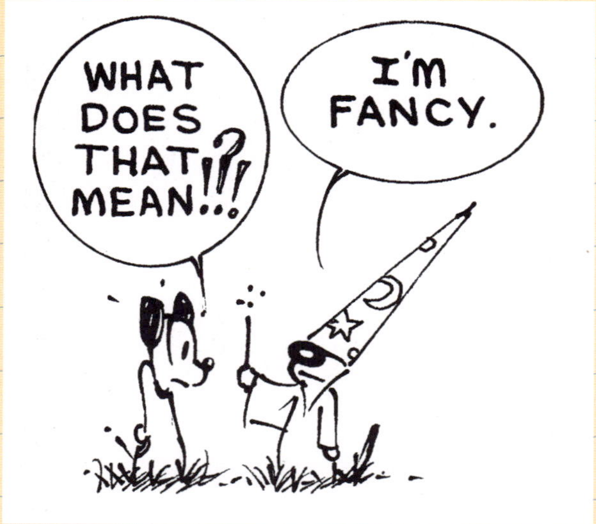
WHAT DOES THAT MEAN!!!?
I'M FANCY.

OH, EARL, MOOCH—I'M IN LOVE—BUT I'M NOT SURE IT'S RIGHT. MY EDWARD IS SO MYSTERIOUS... HE FLIES WITH SUCH GRACE AND HE HAS THE CUTEST WINGS!
BELLA—HE SOUNDS SHPECIAL!
HE IS!
HE'S A BAT.

OH, EDWARD...
WHY CAN'T OUR LOVE BE ACCEPTED?
OH, BELLA...
THE WORLD IS UPSIDE DOWN.

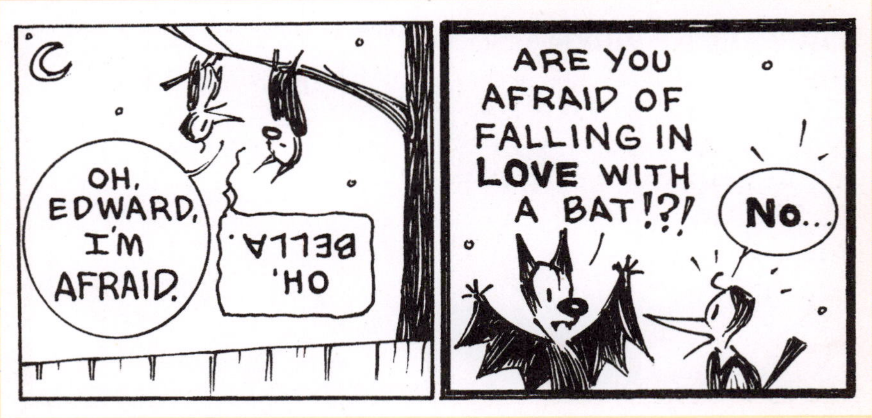
OH, EDWARD, I'M AFRAID.
OH, BELLA.
ARE YOU AFRAID OF FALLING IN **LOVE** WITH A BAT!?!
NO...

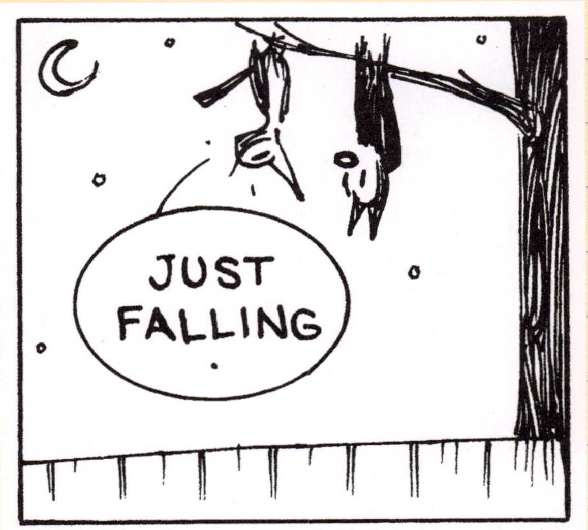
JUST FALLING

OH, BELLA - WHEN YOU ARE WAKING UP TO CATCH THE EARLY WORM - I'M JUST RETURNING TO MY CAVE TO DREAM OF MOONLIT MOSQUITOS!
HOW WILL OUR LOVE SURVIVE!?!
WE CAN DO TAKE-OUT.

OH, BELLA— WHAT DO YOU SEE IN ME— A BAT!?!
OH, EDWARD...
I JUST LIKE HANGING WITH YOU.

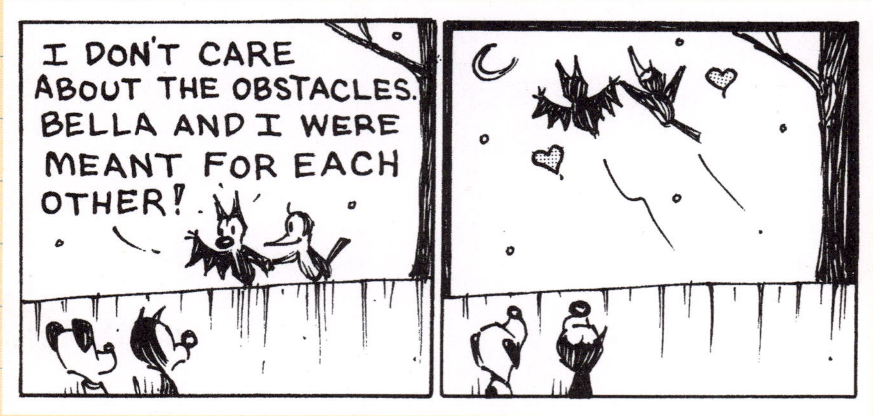
I DON'T CARE ABOUT THE OBSTACLES. BELLA AND I WERE MEANT FOR EACH OTHER!

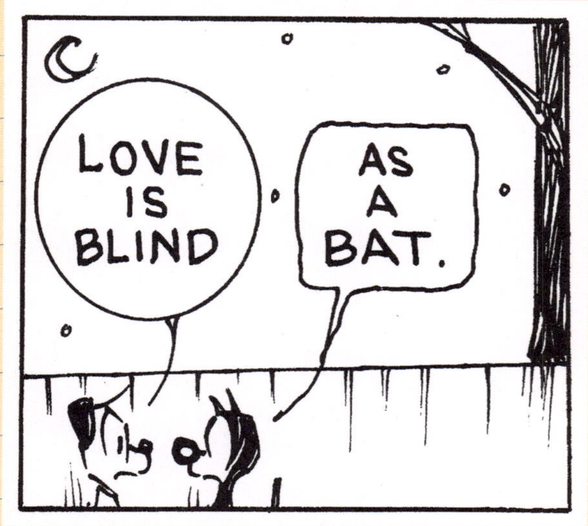
LOVE IS BLIND
AS A BAT.

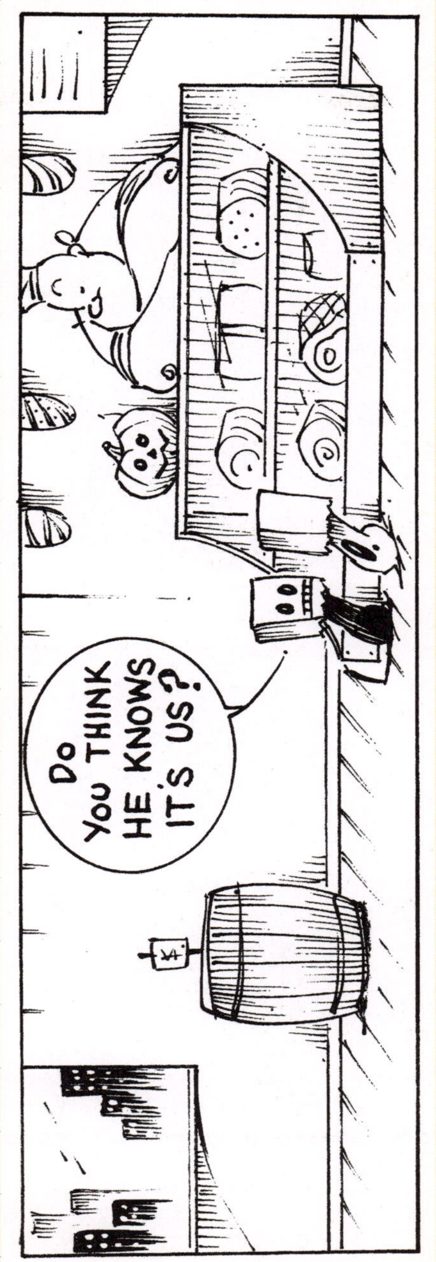
DO YOU THINK HE KNOWS IT'S US?

MY GLASSES ARE THE **LATEST** IN WIZARD WEAR!
NOW I CAN SEE **ALL** AND KNOW **ALL**! A TRUE WIZARD!
LIKE HARRY POTTER

WHO'S THAT?

WITH MY NEW WIZARD GLASSES I CAN SEE IT ALL!

HAVE YOU LOOKED IN A MIRROR LATELY?

I KNOW A FEW TRICKS - SPEAK, SIT, FETCH - DOES THAT MAKE **ME** A WIZARD?
NO.
WHAT DOES?

A SILLY HAT.

OH, PROSPERO— CAN YOU TELL ME THE DIFFERENCE BETWEEN A GOBLIN AND A HOBGOBLIN?
YESH.
FOR ONE...
IT'S A HOBBY.

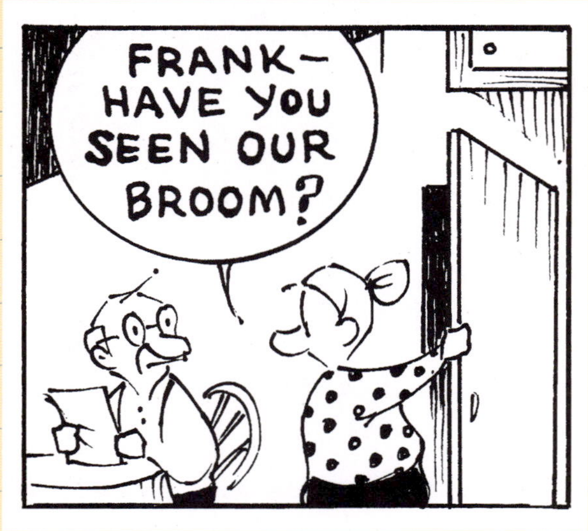
FRANK—
HAVE YOU
SEEN OUR
BROOM?

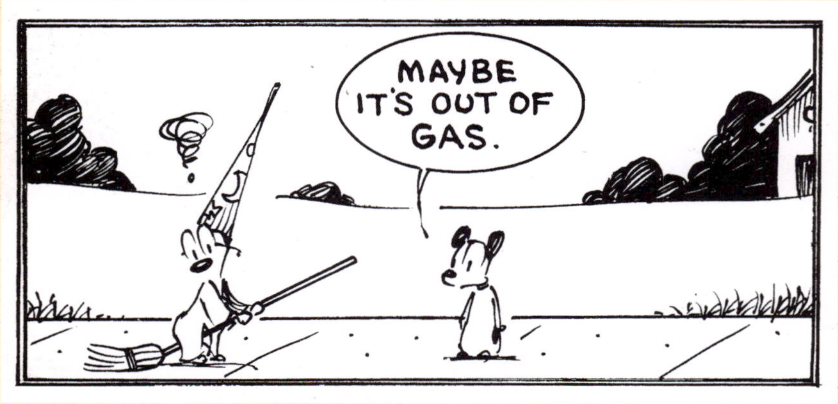
MAYBE
IT'S OUT OF
GAS.

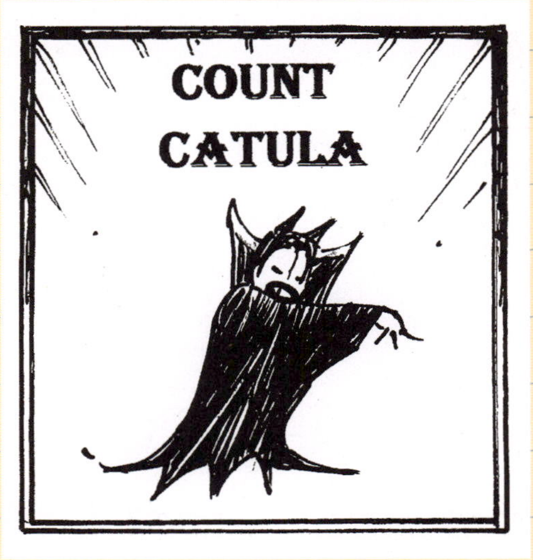
COUNT
CATULA

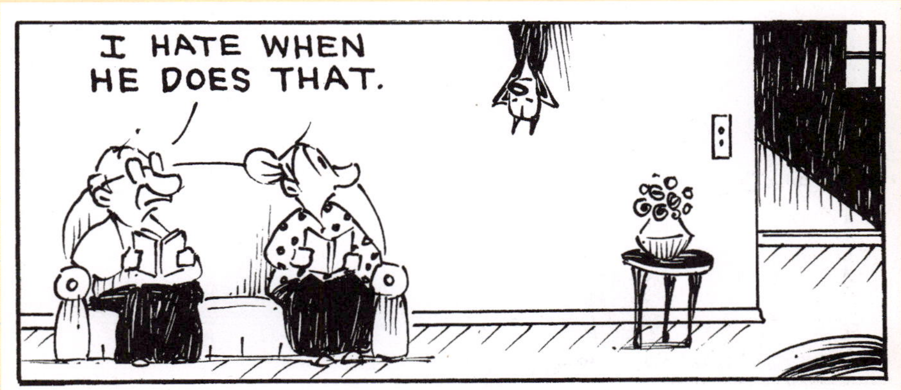
I HATE WHEN HE DOES THAT.

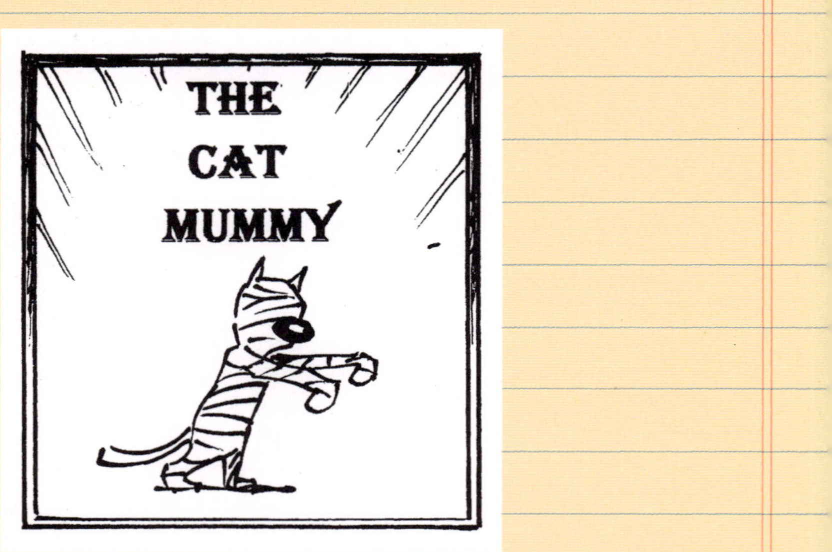
THE CAT MUMMY

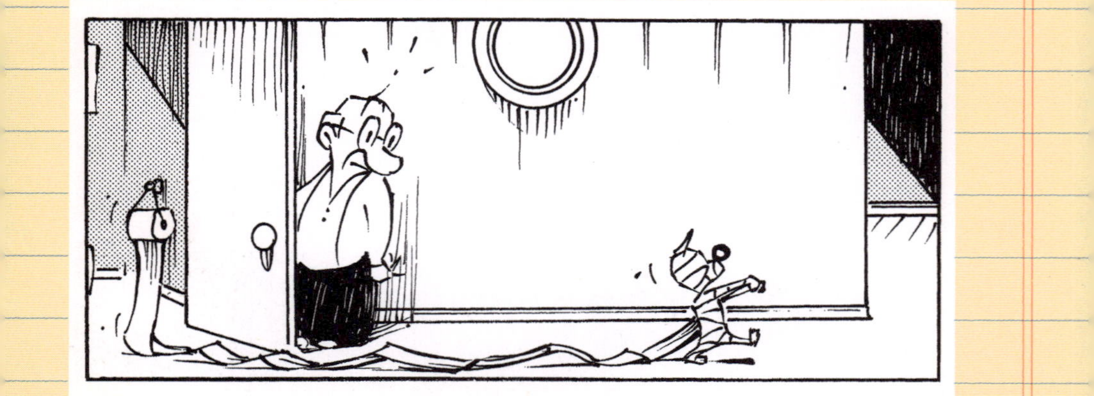

TRICK OR TREAT
DING DONG
HALLOWEEN WAS **TWO** WEEKS AGO!
THAT'S THE TRICK.

TRICK OR TREAT.
KNOCK NOK
WHAT DID YOU GET?
A WART.

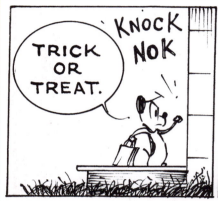

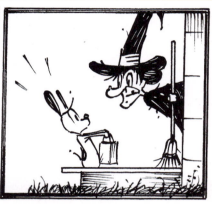

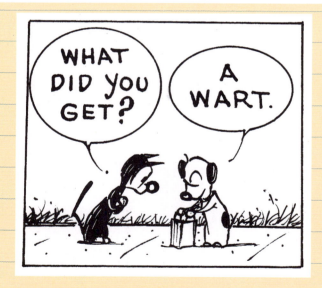

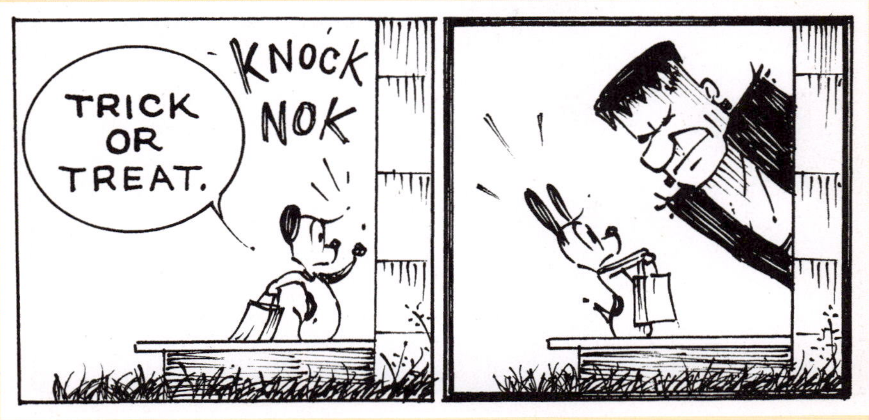
TRICK OR TREAT.
KNOCK NOK

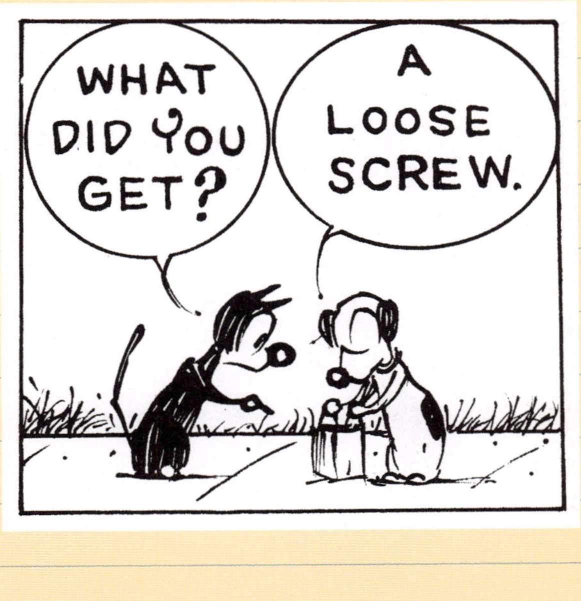
WHAT DID YOU GET?
A LOOSE SCREW.

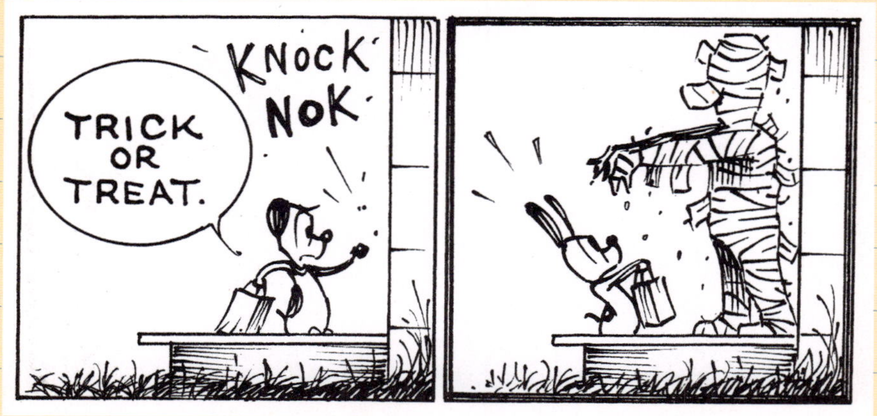
KNOCK
NOK
TRICK OR TREAT.

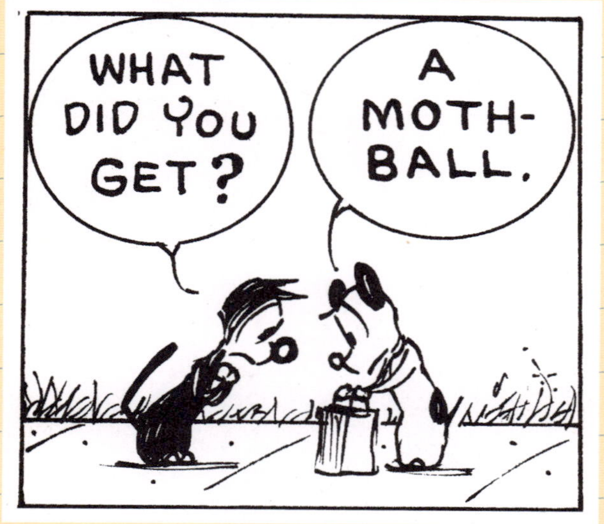
WHAT DID YOU GET?
A MOTH-BALL.

KNOCK
NOK
TRICK OR TREAT.

WHAT DID YOU GET?
A TOASTED MARSH-MALLOW

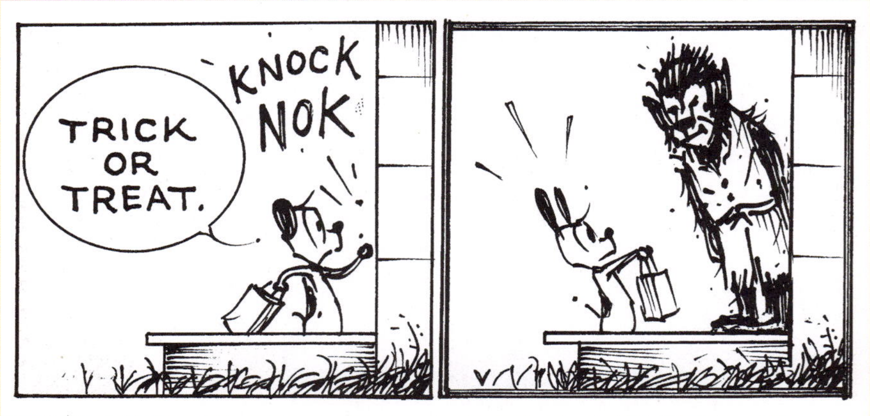
TRICK OR TREAT.
KNOCK NOK

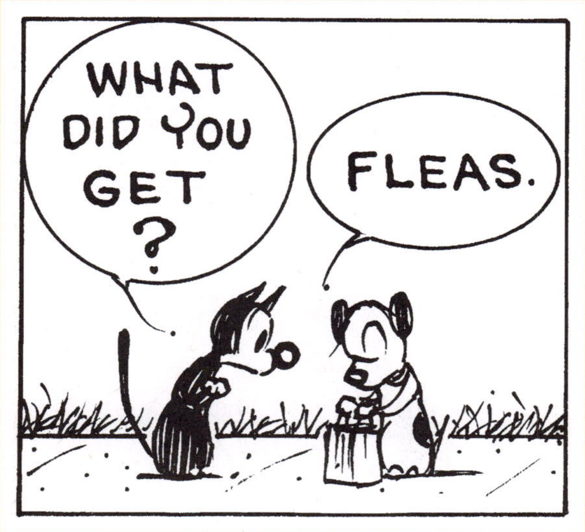
WHAT DID YOU GET ?
FLEAS.

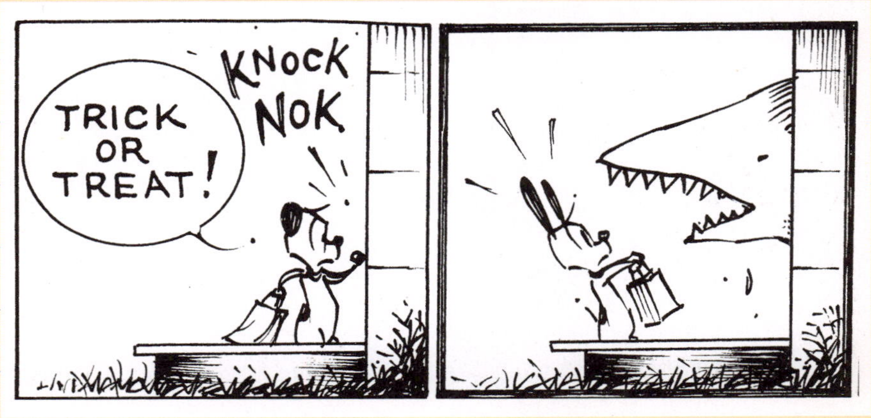
TRICK OR TREAT!
KNOCK NOK

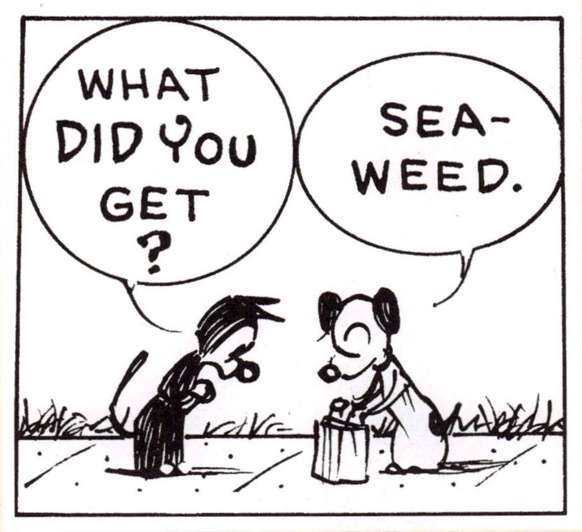
WHAT DID YOU GET?
SEA-WEED.

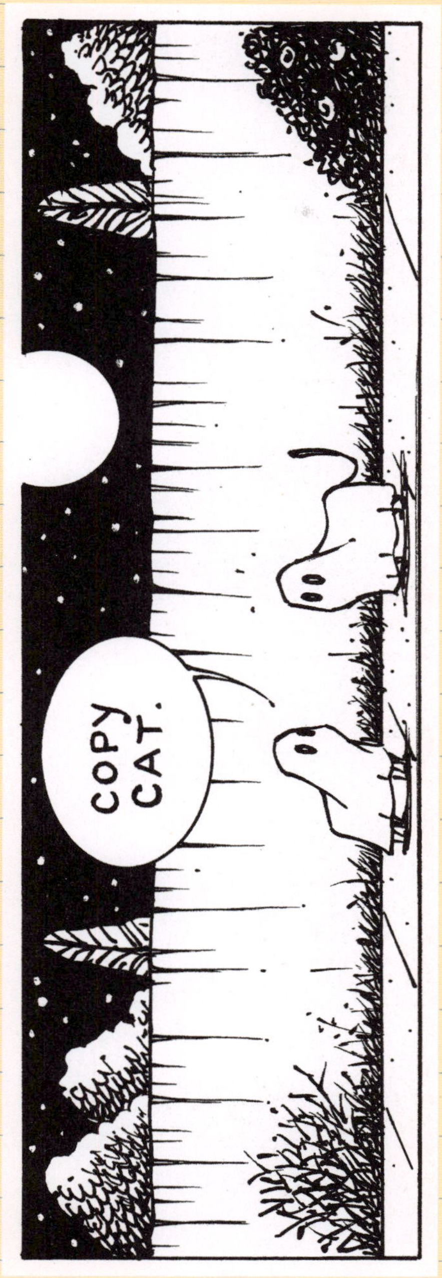
COPY
CAT.

POOF!
THE GREAT PROSHPERO HAS RETURNED!
WHAT MAGICAL WIZARDRY SHALL I PERFORM FOR YOU?

CAN HE MAKE HIMSELF DISAPPEAR?

I WILL PERFORM THE ULTIMATE DISHAPPEARING ACT!
SHIM
SHA-LA
BIM!

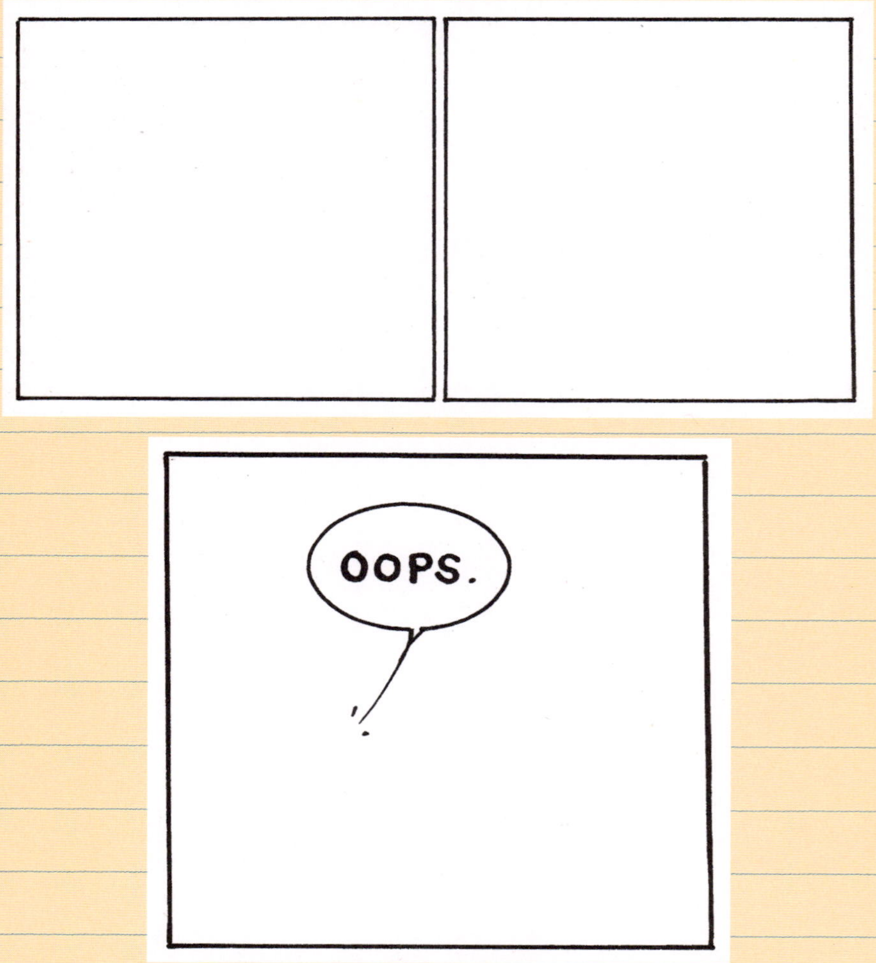
OOPS.

MOOCH! CAN YOU USE YOUR CAT MAGIC TO MAKE US REAPPEAR !?!
OF COURSE I CAN.
THANK GOOD-NESS!
DO YOU SEE MY MAGIC WAND ANY-WHERE?

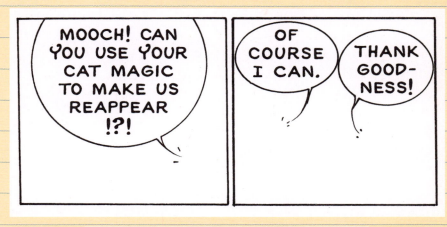

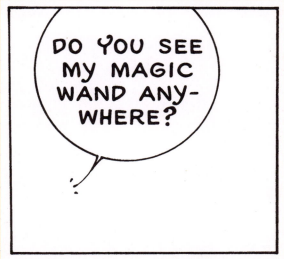

OK, EARL, HERE GOES A LITTLE HOCUSH-POCUSH TO BRING US BACK!
BIM
SHA-LA
SHIM!

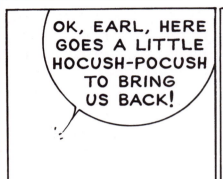

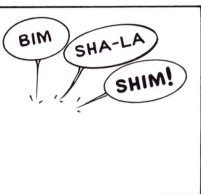

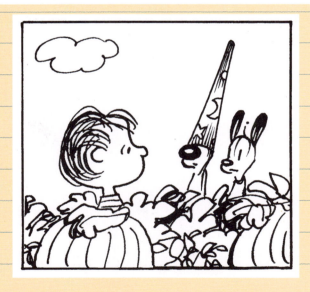

SORRY, EARL. I GUESSH I NEED TO FOCUS ON MY HOCUS-POCUS.
IT'S OK, MOOCH. NO MATTER HOW MUCH TROUBLE YOU GET US INTO, YOU ALWAYS MAKE IT ENJOYABLE.

YESH
THAT'S MY BEST TRICK.

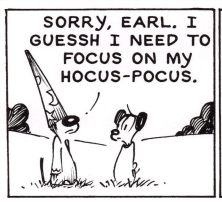

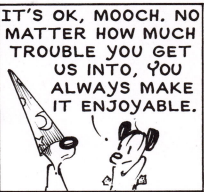

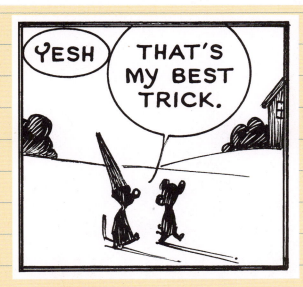

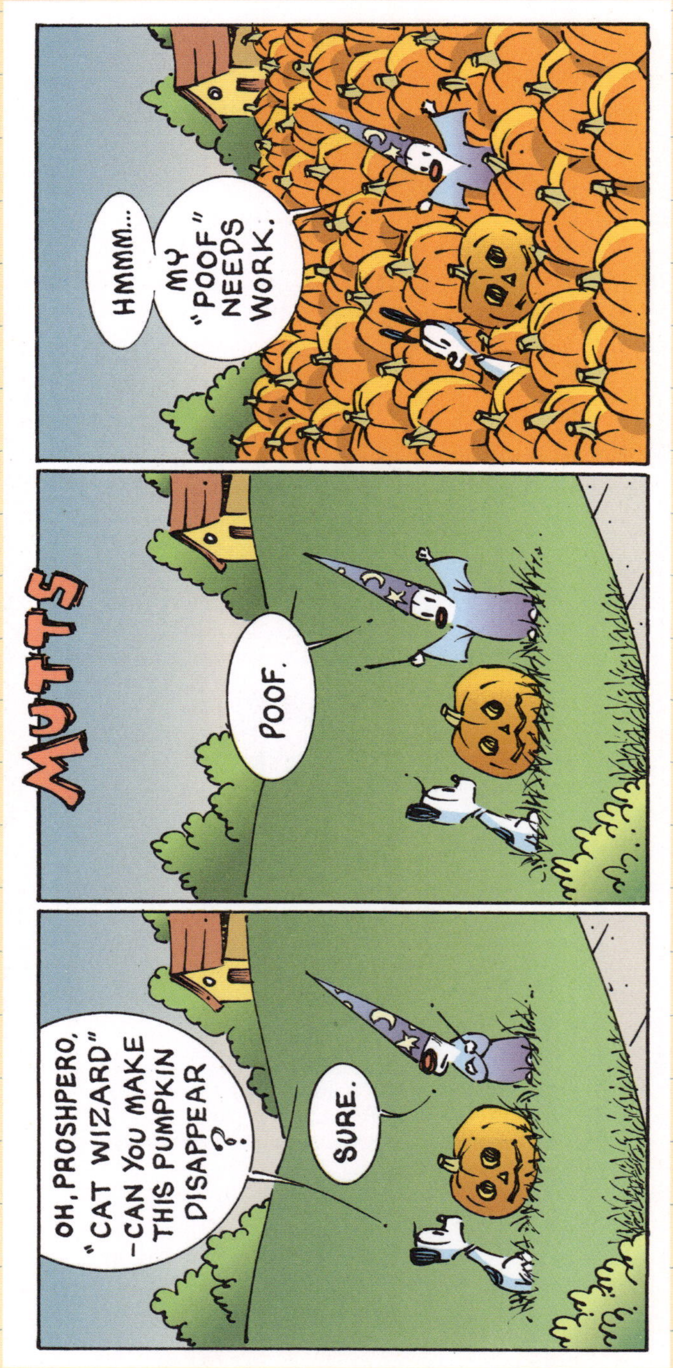
MUTTS
OH, PROSHPERO, "CAT WIZARD" —CAN YOU MAKE THIS PUMPKIN DISAPPEAR ?
SURE.
POOF.
HMMM...
MY "POOF" NEEDS WORK.

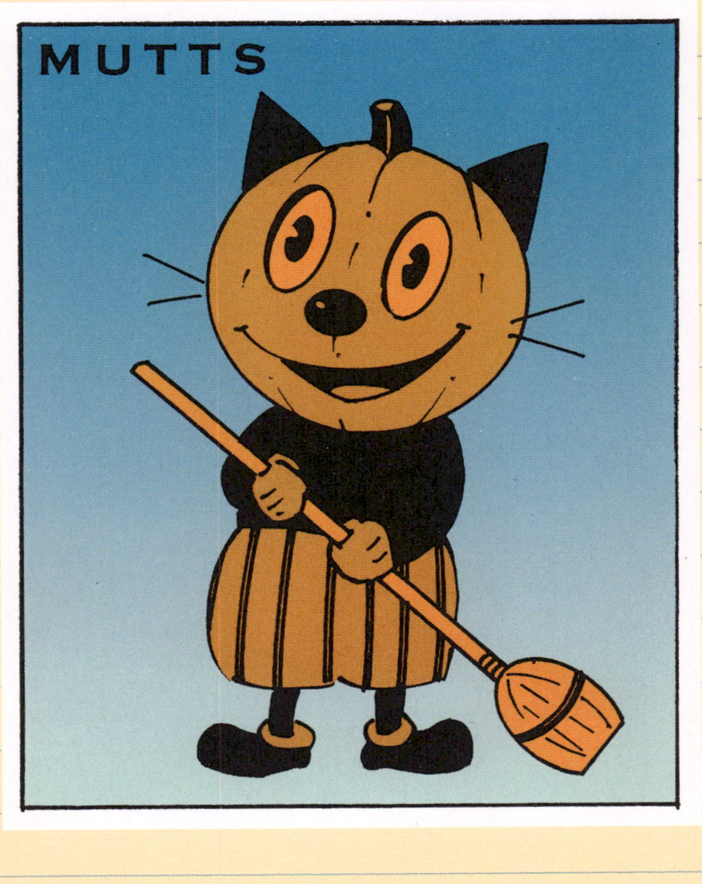
MUTTS

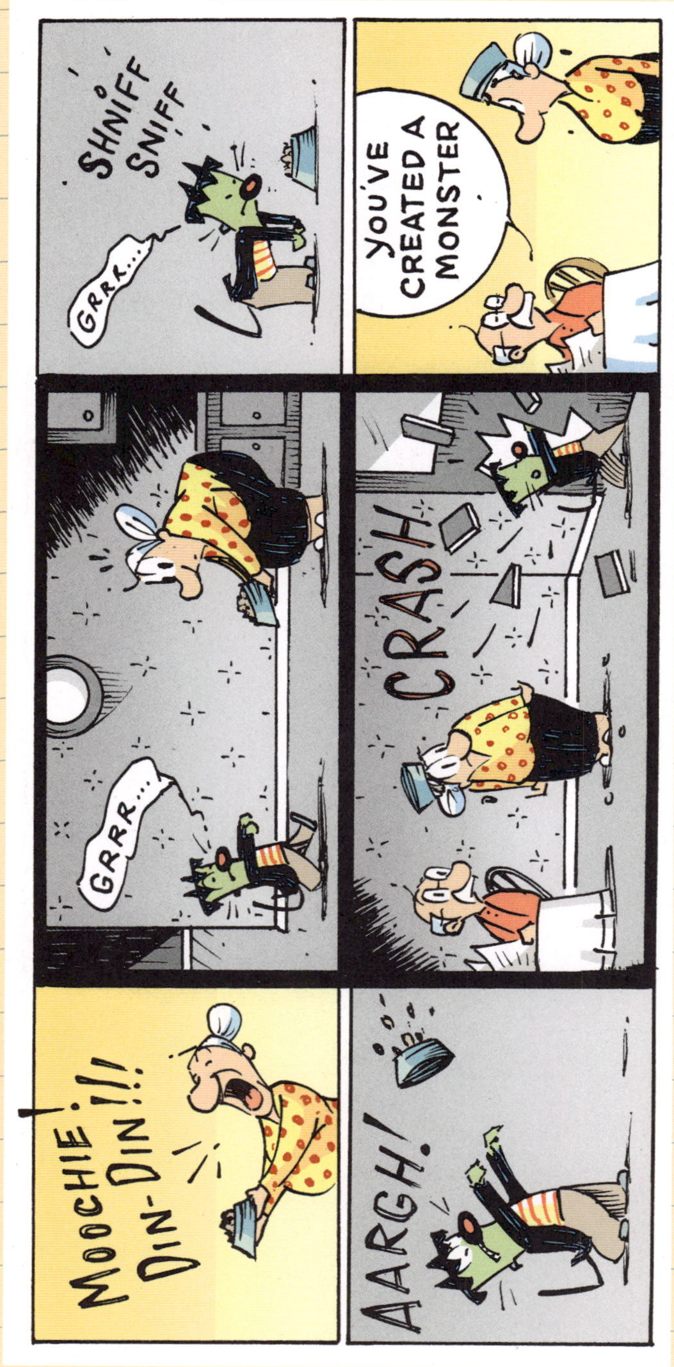
MOOCHIE! DIN-DIN!!!
GRRR...
GRRR...
SHNIFF SNIFF
AARGH!
CRASH
YOU'VE CREATED A MONSTER

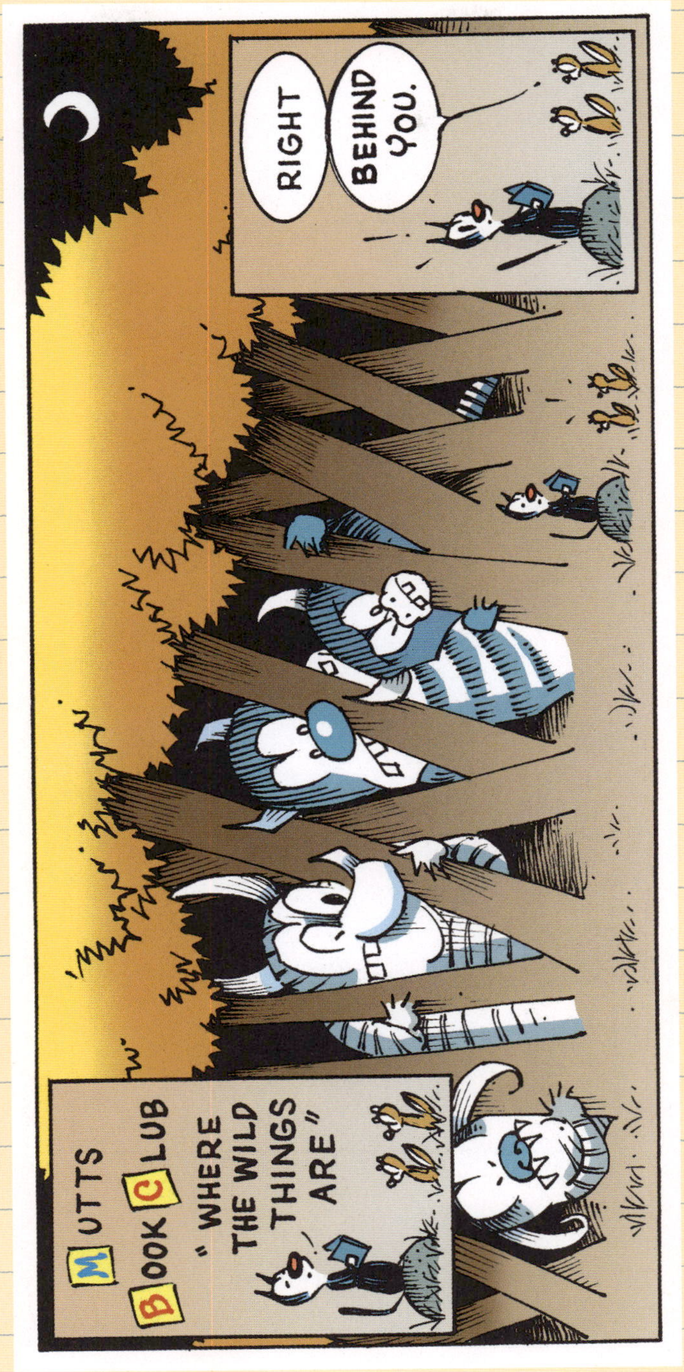
MUTTS BOOK CLUB
"WHERE THE WILD THINGS ARE"
RIGHT
BEHIND YOU.

WHERE'S PHILIPPE?
SOUTH.
ALL THE BIRDS GOT UP AND LEFT.
?

WAS IT SHOMETHING I SAID ?

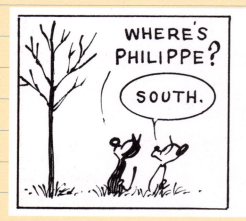

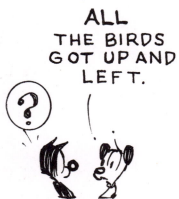

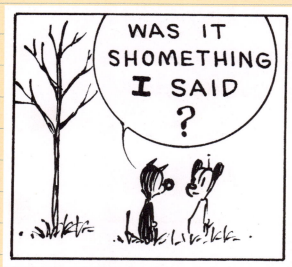

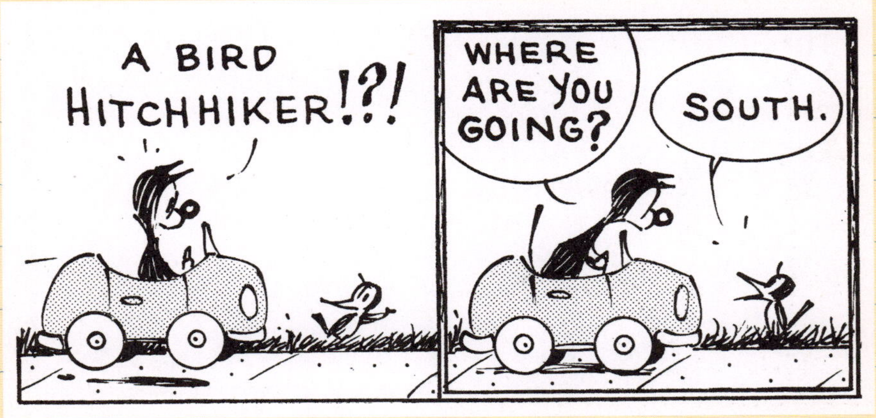
A BIRD HITCHHIKER!?!
WHERE ARE YOU GOING?
SOUTH.

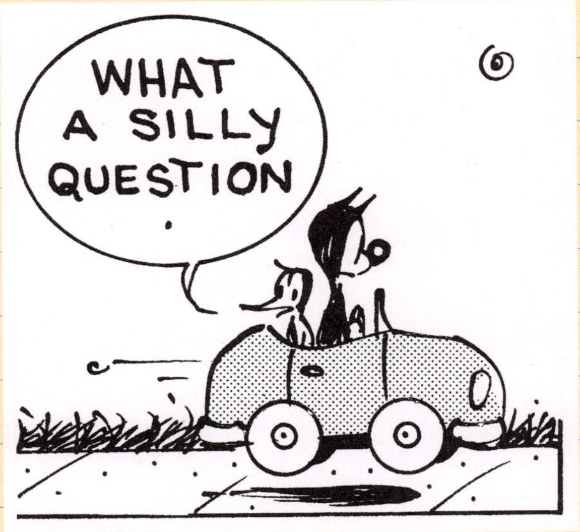
WHAT A SILLY QUESTION

HEY, FROGGY, ARE YOU GOING SOUTH TO SPEND THE WINTER PLAYING ON WARM BEACHES LIKE THE BIRDS?
NO, MY GOOD FRIEND, I'M GOING TO SPEND IT SLEEPING UNDER THIS MUD.

YOU NEED A NEW AGENT.
!

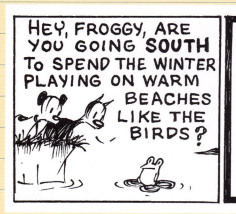

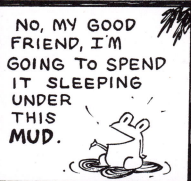

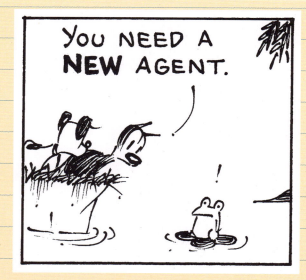

A HONEY-GLAZED PEANUT.
BONK
SWEET.

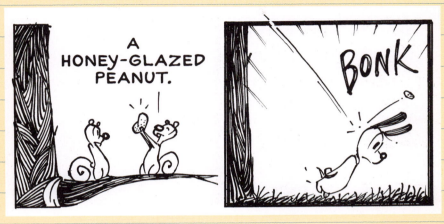

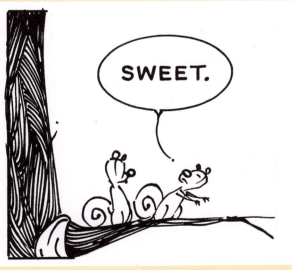

SUMMER'S OFFICIALLY OVER.
I FEEL RIDICULOUS.

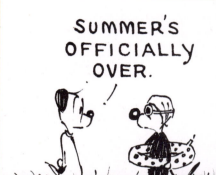

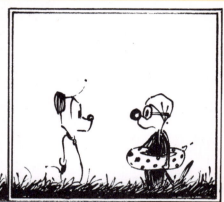

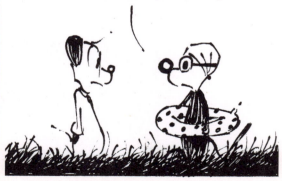

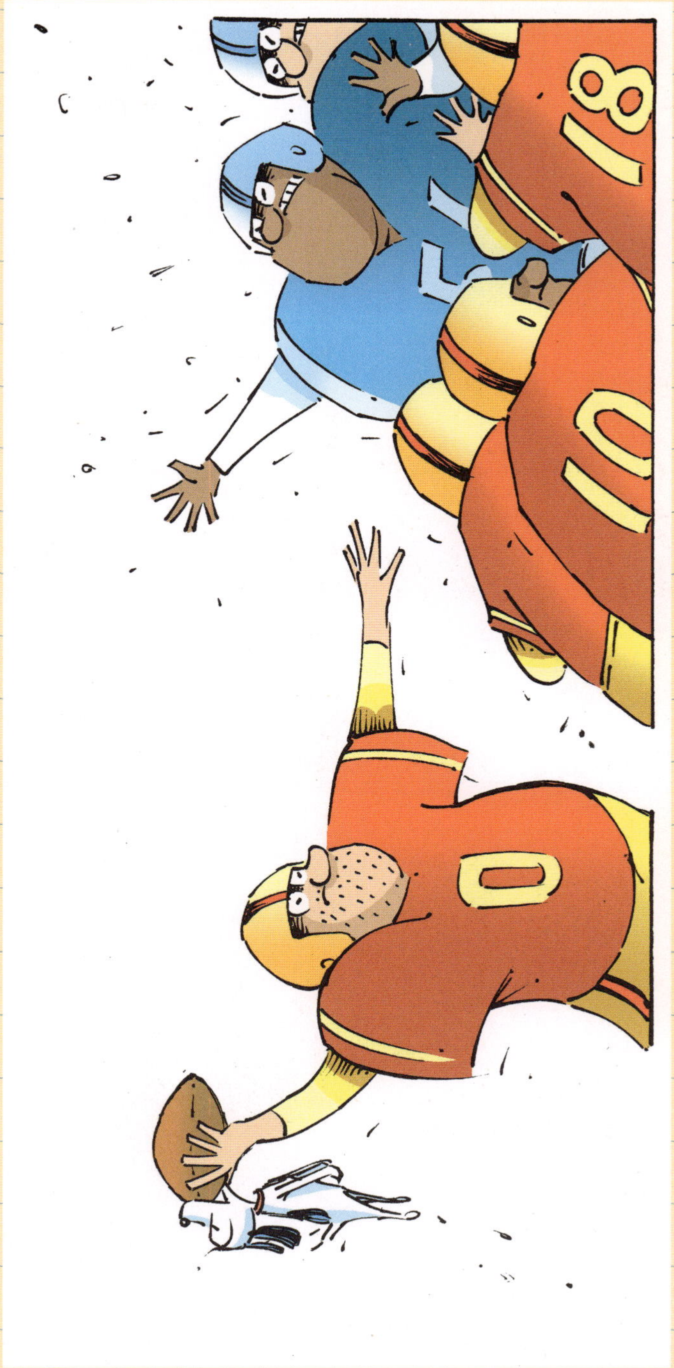

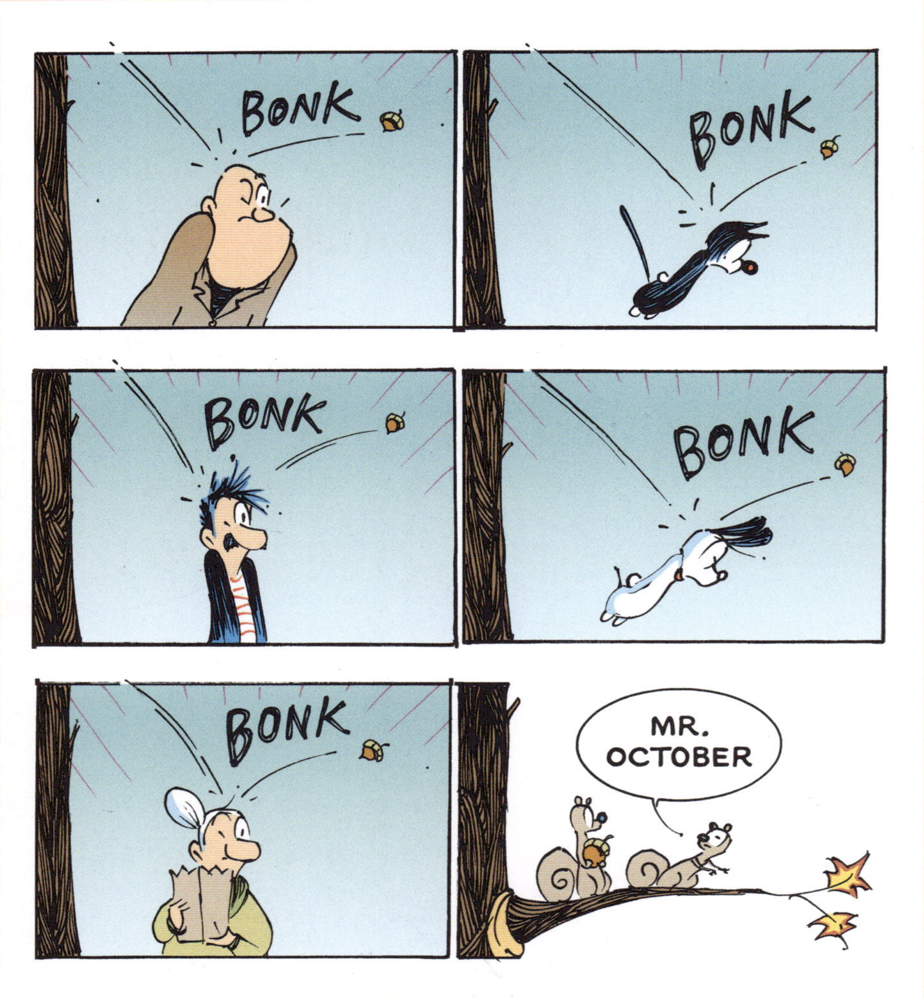
BONK
BONK
BONK
BONK
BONK
MR. OCTOBER

Y'KNOW, IT STILL FEELS LIKE SUMMER VACATION TO ME.
BUT I THINK I'M FINALLY ADJUSTING TO THE WHOLE "BACK TO SCHOOL" THING.

TODAY'S SATURDAY.

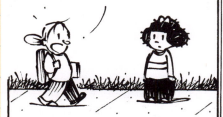

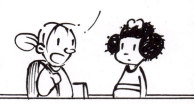

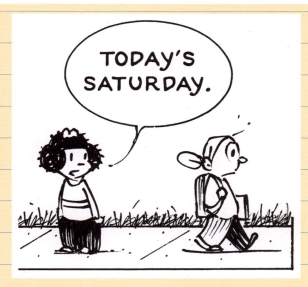

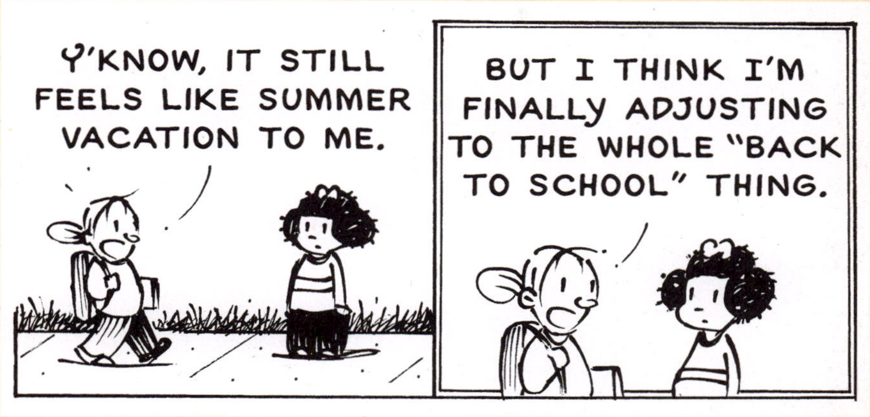

PING
PING
PING
POK
PING
PING
POK
PING

THAT'S THE PROBLEM WITH PEANUTS— ONCE YOU START YOU CAN'T STOP!

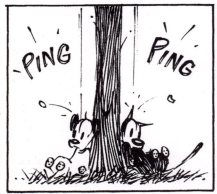

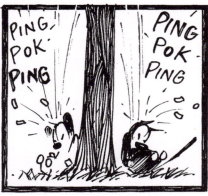

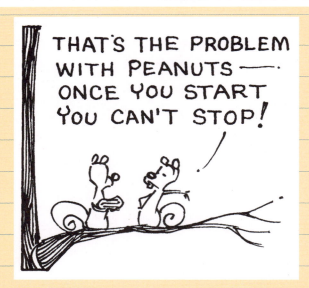

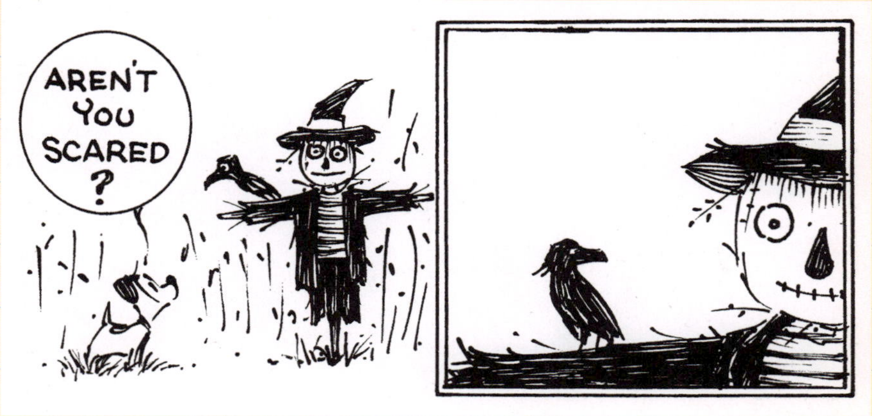
AREN'T YOU SCARED?

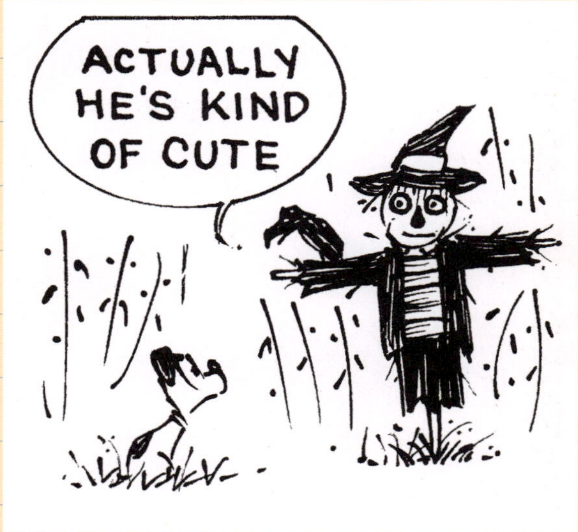
ACTUALLY HE'S KIND OF CUTE

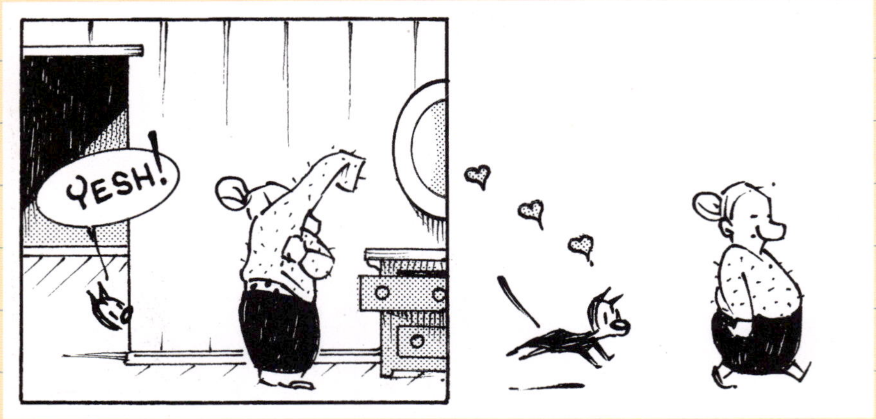
YESH!

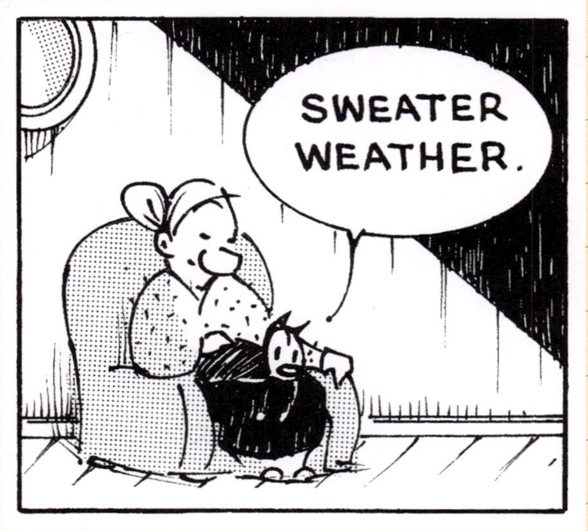
SWEATER
WEATHER.

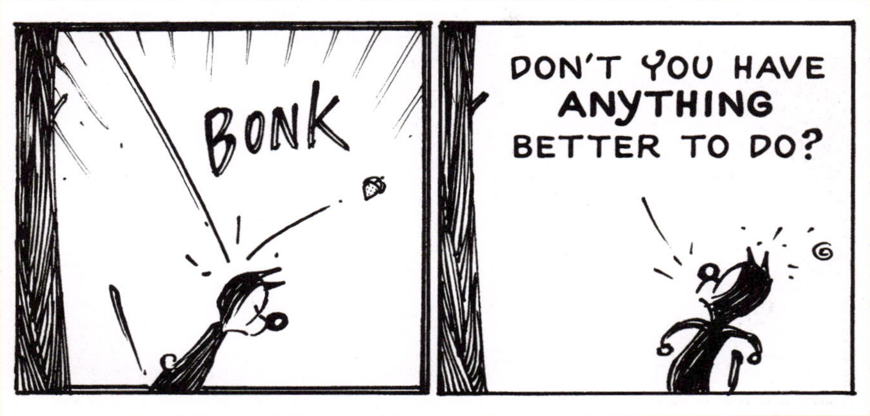
BONK
DON'T YOU HAVE ANYTHING BETTER TO DO?

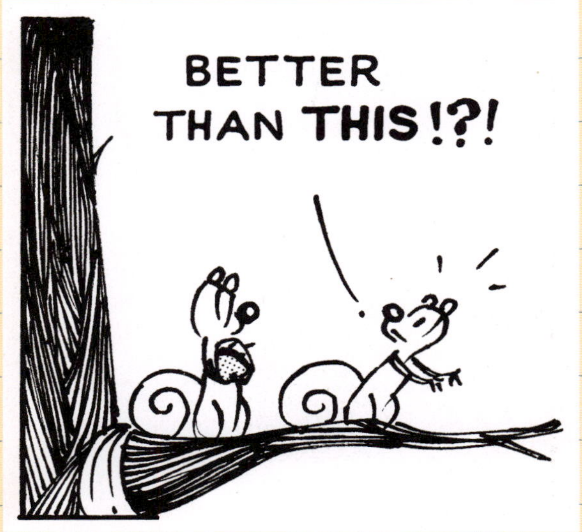
BETTER THAN THIS!?!

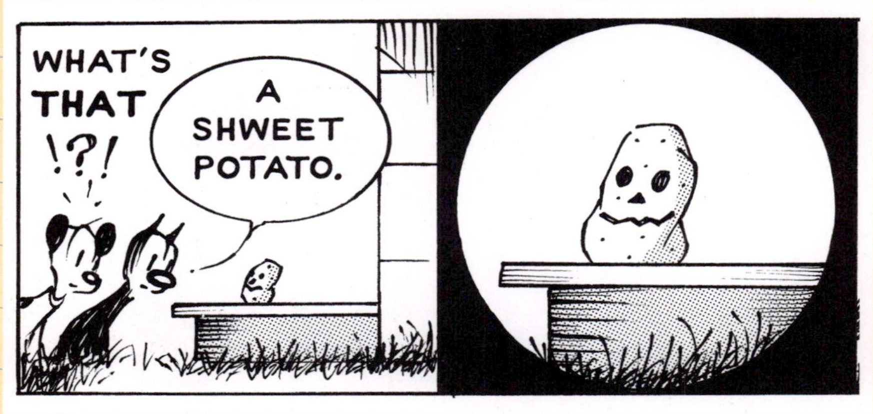
WHAT'S THAT !?!
A SHWEET POTATO.

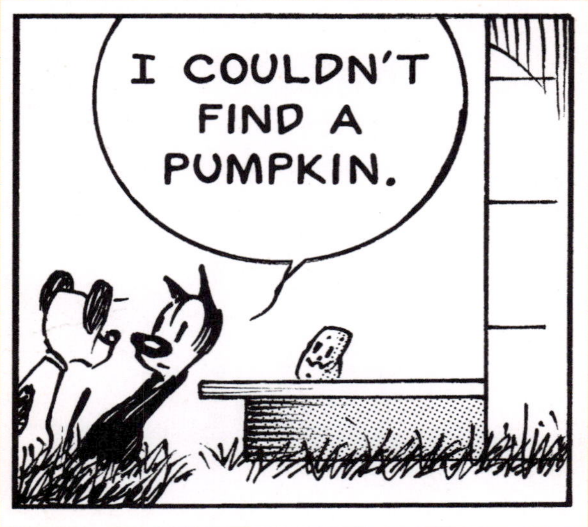
I COULDN'T FIND A PUMPKIN.

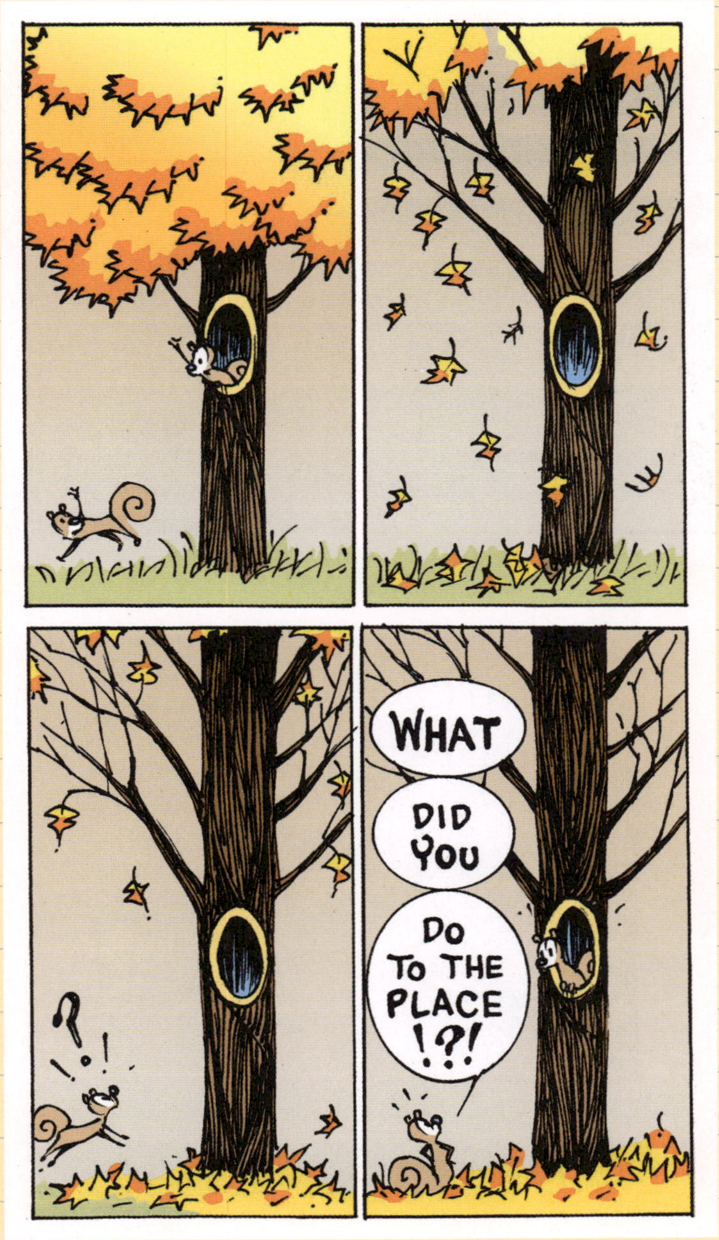
WHAT
DID YOU
DO TO THE PLACE !?!

BONK
SHAKE
SHAKE

NUTS
SALTED

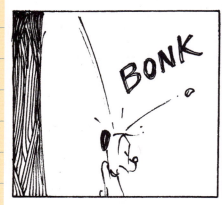

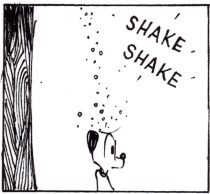

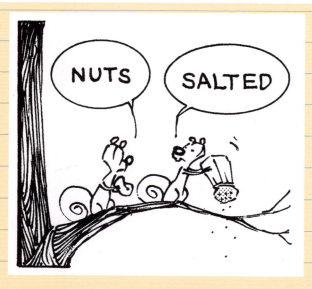

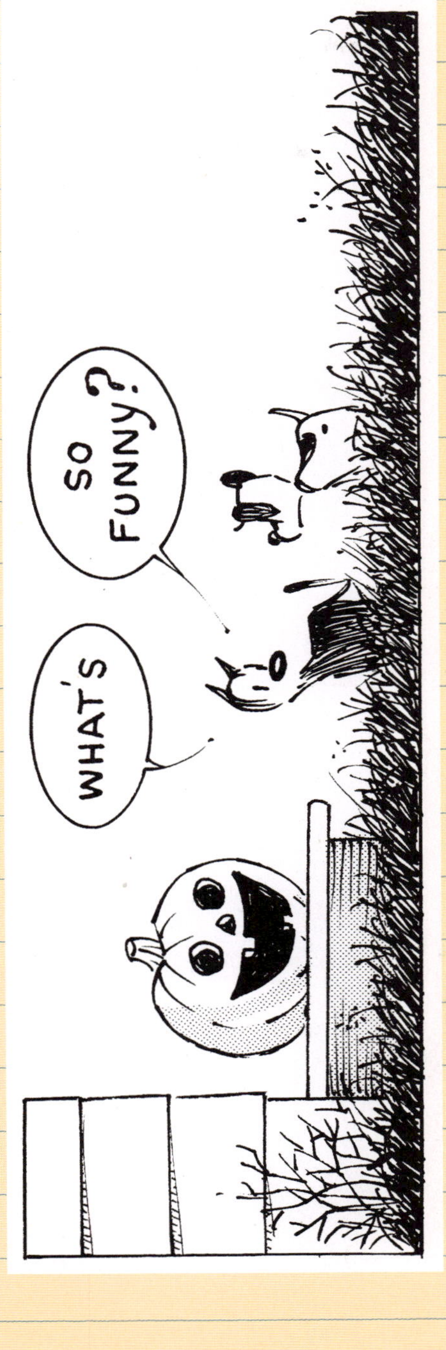
WHAT'S
SO FUNNY?

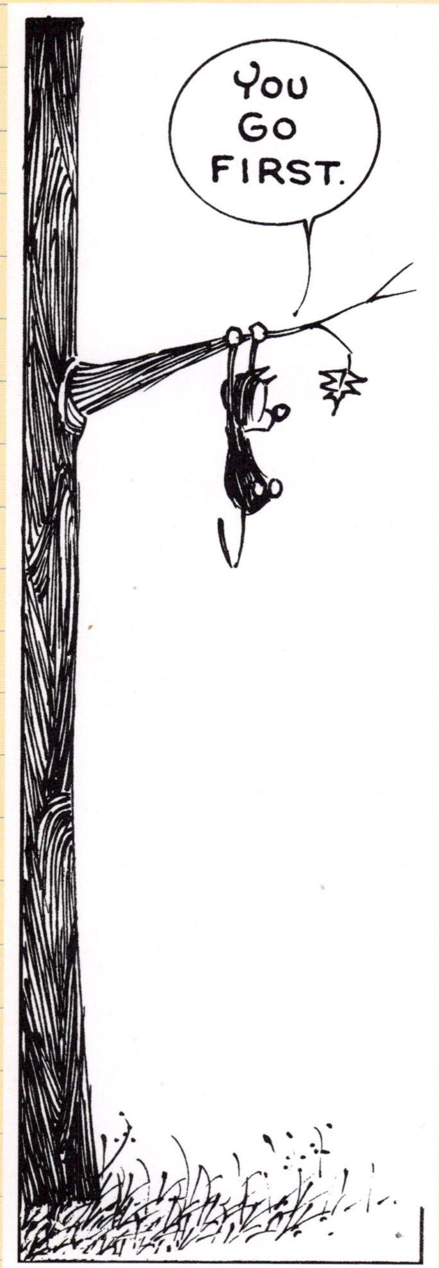
YOU GO FIRST.

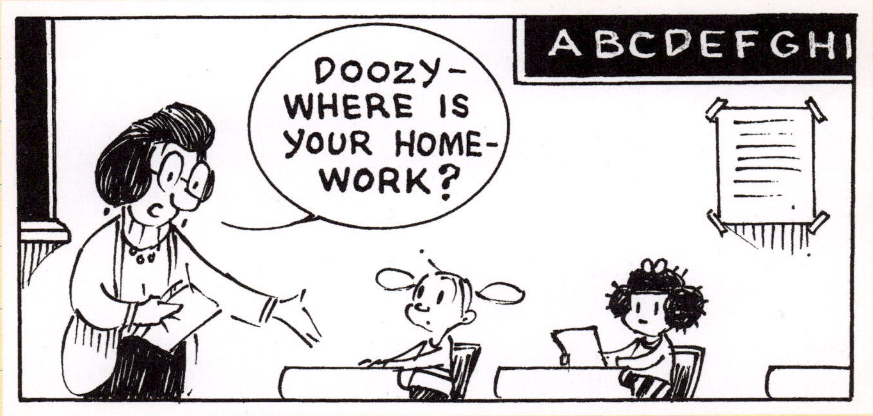
ABCDEFGHI
DOOZY- WHERE IS YOUR HOME-WORK?

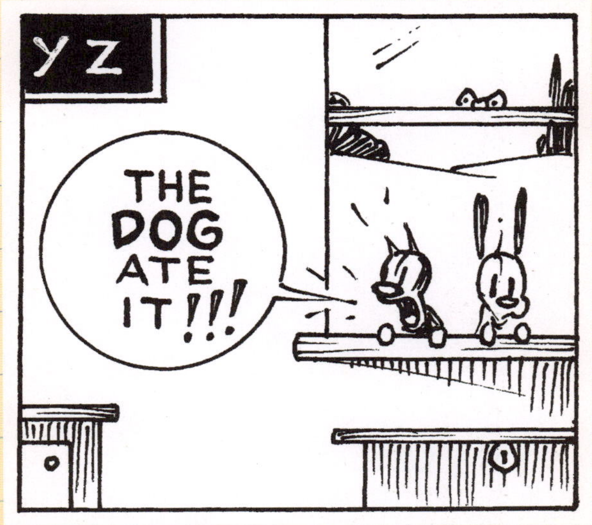
YZ
THE DOG ATE IT!!!

SHELTER STORIES UPDATE

"TOM-TOM"

I'M CELEBRATING MY NINTH YEAR OF ADOPTION.

NINE WONDERFUL YEARS WITH MY FAMILY.

I KNEW I WAS A **KEEPER**!

HERE! HERE! ME! ME!!!
BONK

HE WAS OPEN.

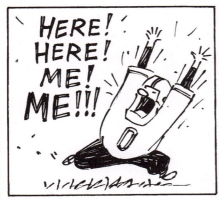

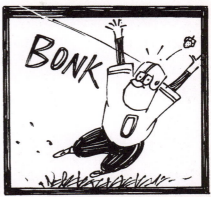

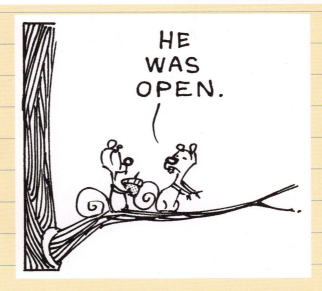

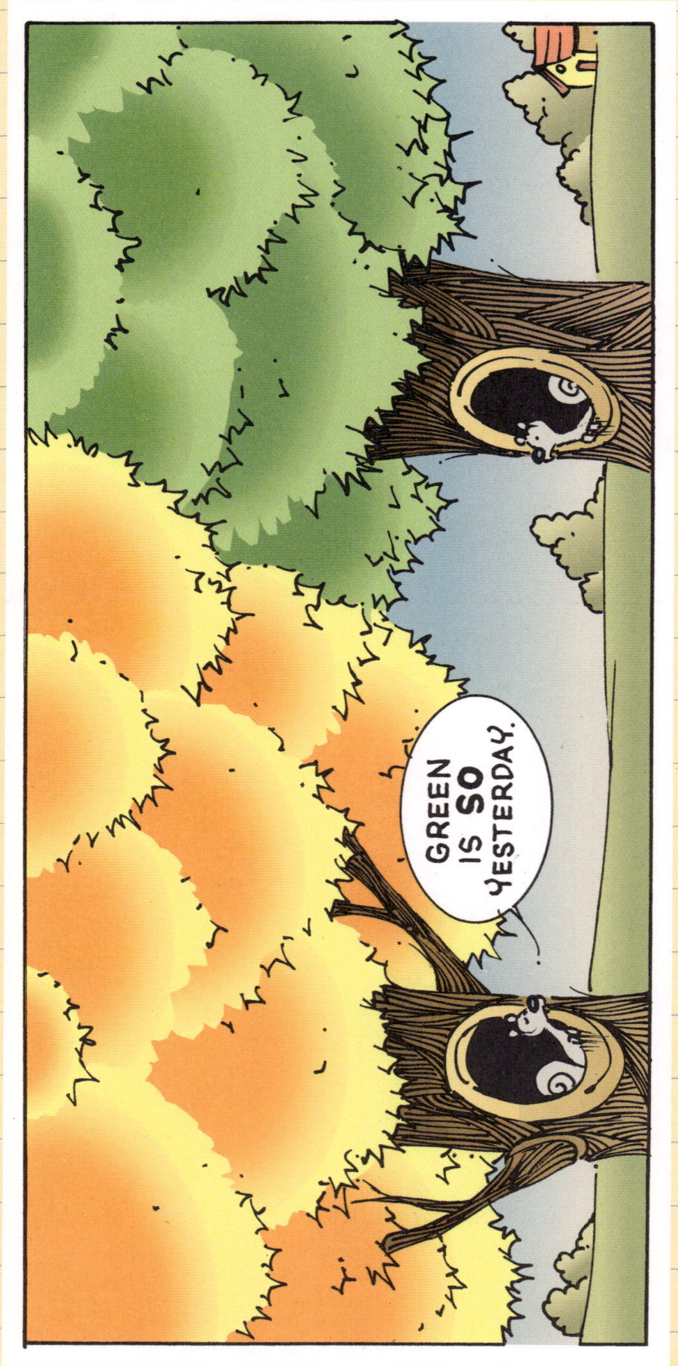
GREEN IS SO YESTERDAY.

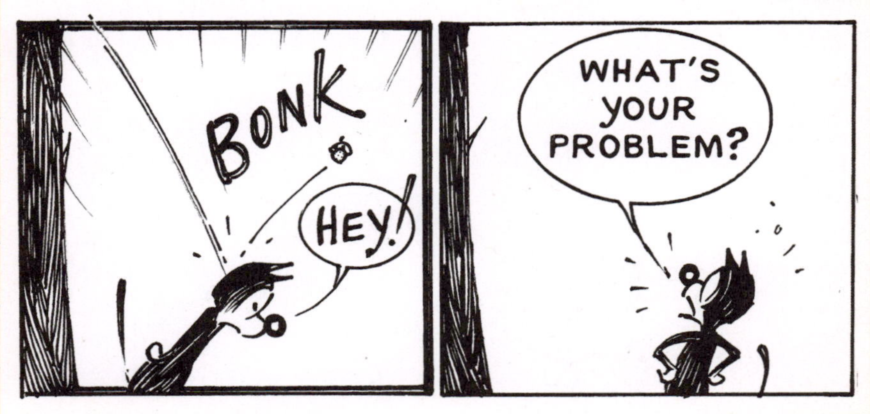
BONK
HEY!
WHAT'S YOUR PROBLEM?

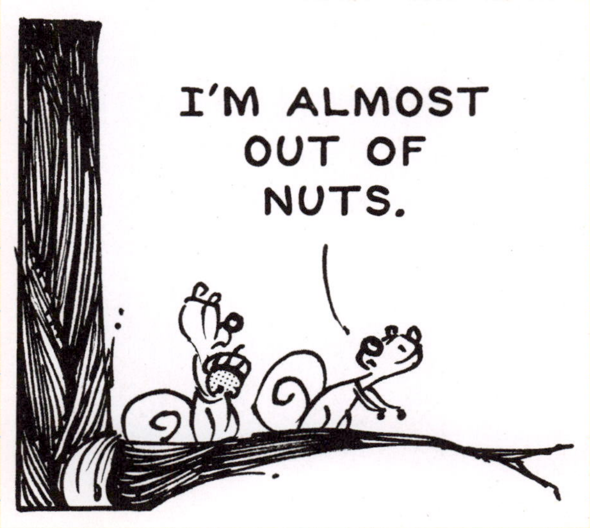
I'M ALMOST OUT OF NUTS.

GRRRR...
HEY, MOOCH, WHAT'S THE MATTER?

THIS KID WON'T SHTOP SHTARING AT ME.

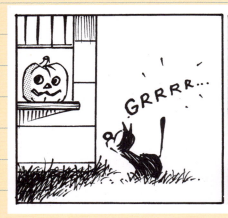

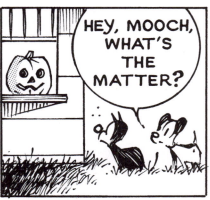

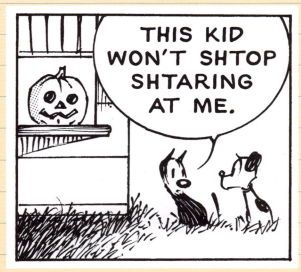

TRICK OR TREAT?
TREAT!
WE'RE FOSTERING A KITTY!

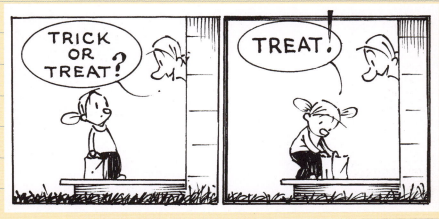

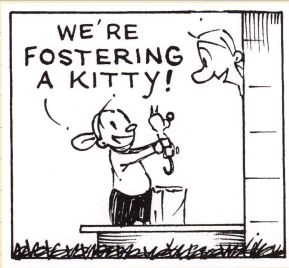

WELCOME TO YOUR NEW FOSTER HOME!
MI CASA ES SU CASA
?

HABLA ESPAÑOL?

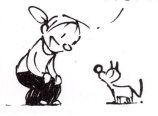

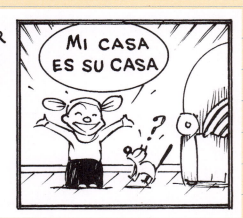

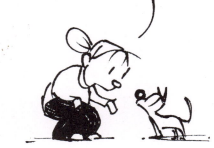

OUR FAMILY IS FOSTERING A KITTY!

HE GETS TO LIVE AT OUR HOUSE UNTIL THE SHELTER FINDS HIM A FOREVER HOME.

KISS!

Shelter Stories

"FLASH"

I'm a greyhound, a racing greyhound.

I spent the first three years of my life either in a cage or out racing. Racing, racing, racing.

I always lost.

I was determined 'useless' and was to be 'weeded out.'

Then a greyhound rescue group saved me and found me a loving home and family.

I raced to their open arms.

I finally won.

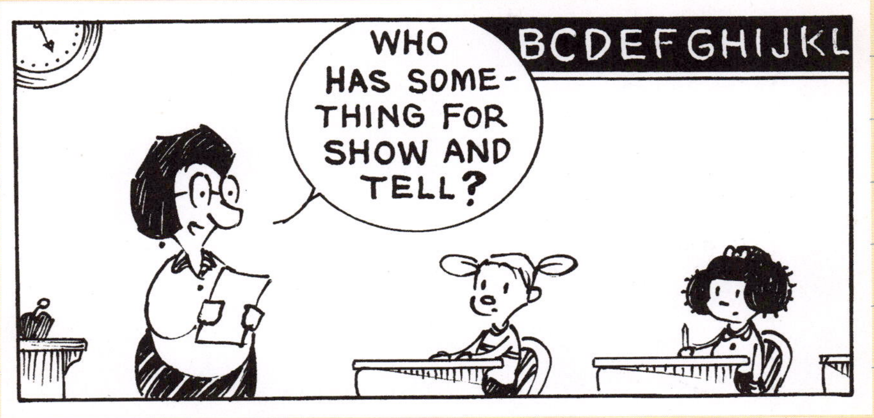
BCDEFGHIJKL
WHO HAS SOME-THING FOR SHOW AND TELL?

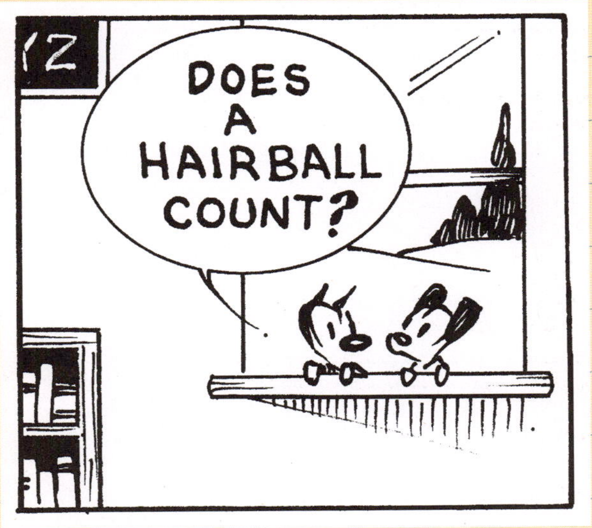
DOES A HAIRBALL COUNT?

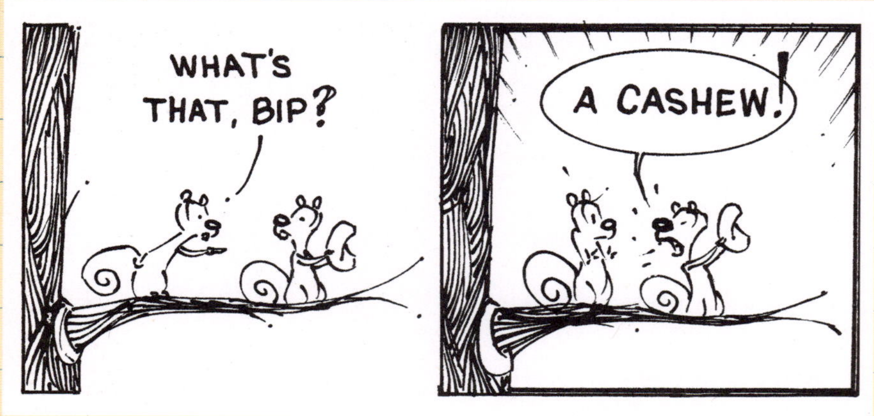
WHAT'S THAT, BIP?
A CASHEW!

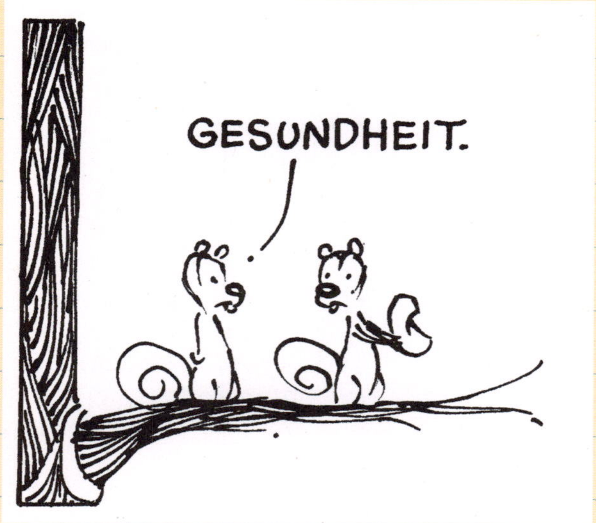
GESUNDHEIT.

GIMME AN 'S'- GIMME AN 'O' - GIMME A 'U' GIMME A 'T' - GIMME AN 'H'!
GO SOUTH!
A CHEERLEADER'S WORK IS NEVER DONE.

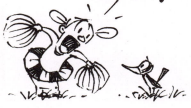

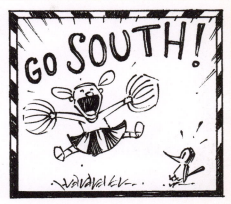

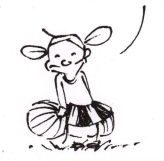

EARL,
DID YOU EVER NOTICE-
PUMPKINS ARE THE HAPPIEST VEGETABLES.

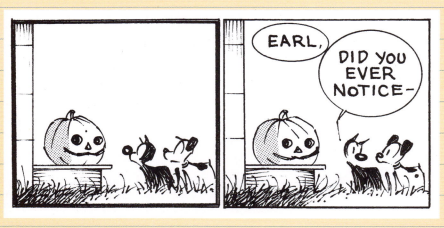

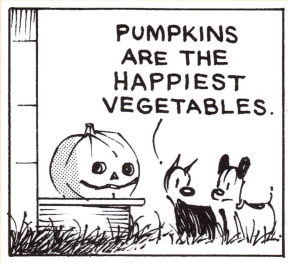

SHELTER STORIES
"EDDIE·DO"
YUP...I LEARNED TO GET AROUND ON THREE LEGS.
No BIG DEAL.
I WONDER HOW YOU MANAGE ON JUST TWO.

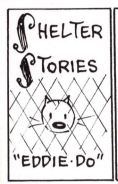

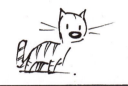

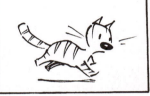

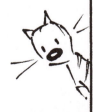

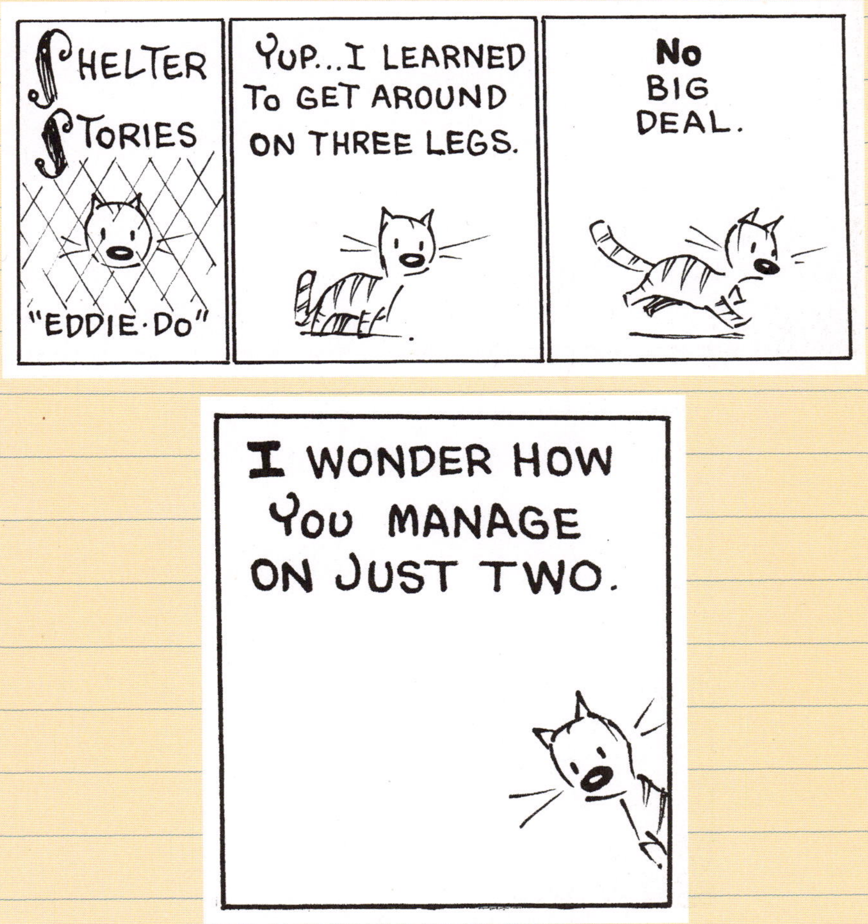

PHILIPPE'S TO DO LIST
HEAD SOUTH

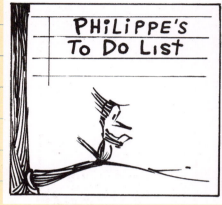

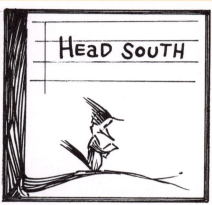

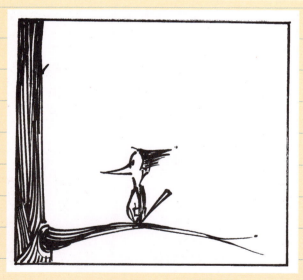

WE'VE BEEN INVADED.

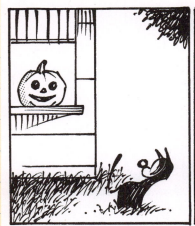

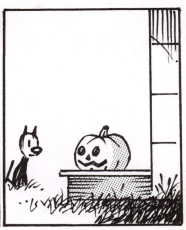

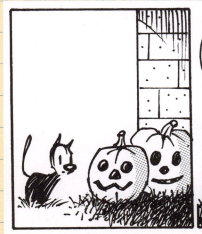

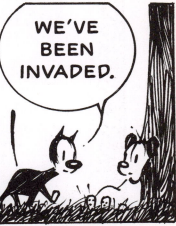

JUST KICKIN'
YESH

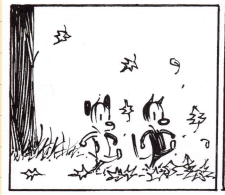

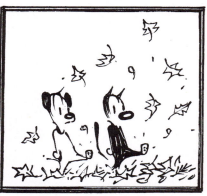

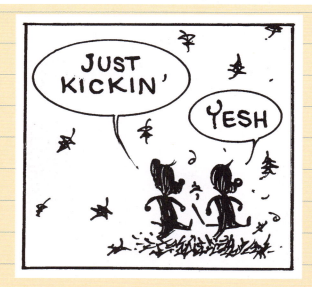

I THOUGHT YOU WENT SOUTH!?!
I CAME BACK FOR AN ENCORE.

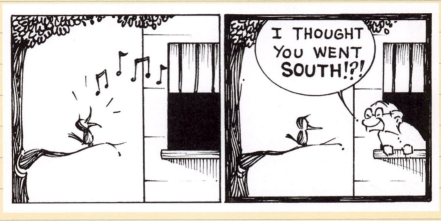

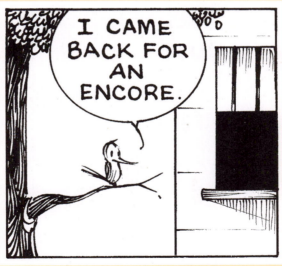

SHELTER STORIES

"BUBULA"

YOU COULD GO TO YOUR SHELTER AND THEY MIGHT HAVE A HAMSTER.

AND YOU COULD BRING THAT HAMSTER TO YOUR HAPPY HOME!

IT'S **ALL** IN **YOUR** HANDS.

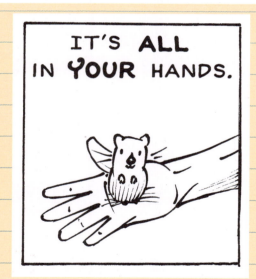

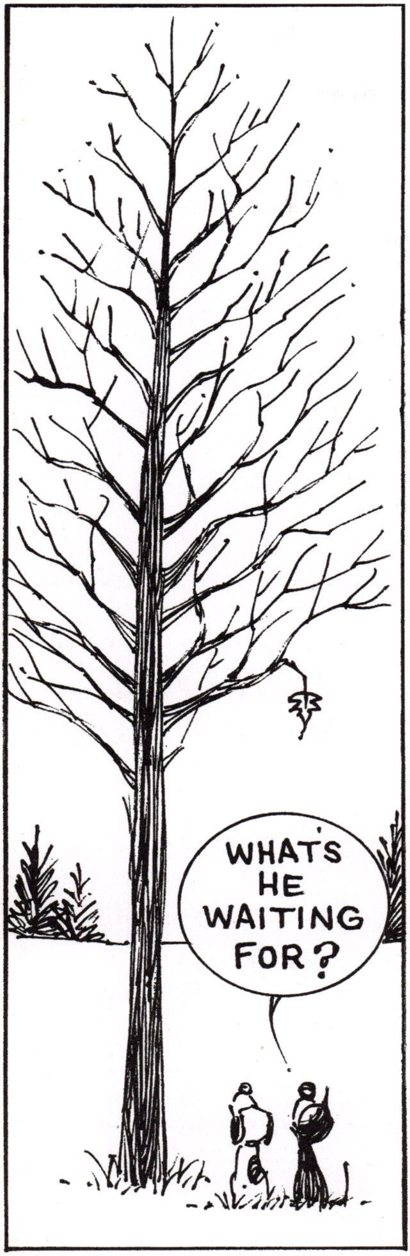
WHAT'S HE WAITING FOR?

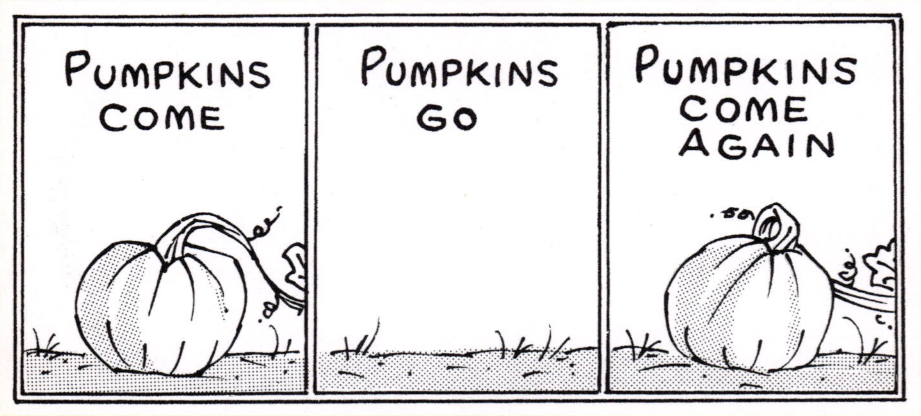
PUMPKINS COME
PUMPKINS GO
PUMPKINS COME AGAIN

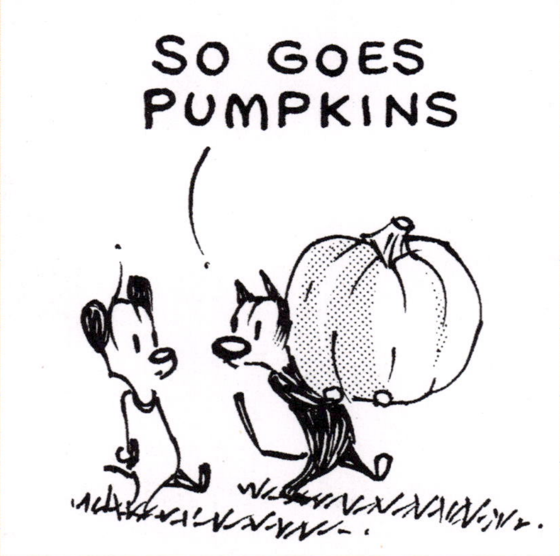
SO GOES PUMPKINS

YOU KNOW WHAT'S FUN IN AUTUMN, MOOCH?—A HAYRIDE!
YESH
I DON'T GET IT.

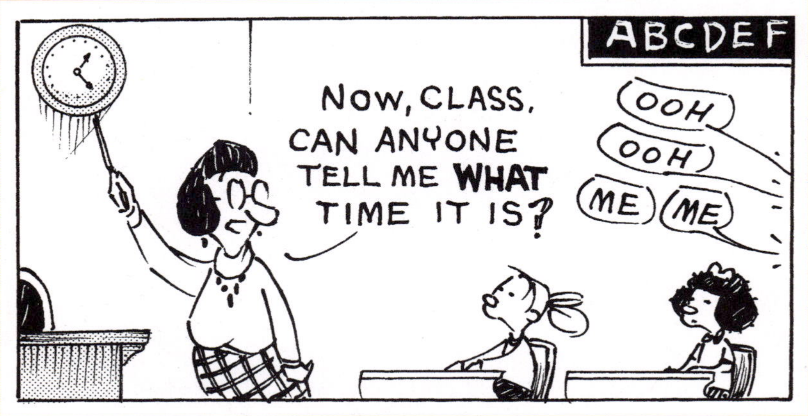
ABCDEF
NOW, CLASS, CAN ANYONE TELL ME **WHAT** TIME IT IS?
OOH
OOH
ME
ME

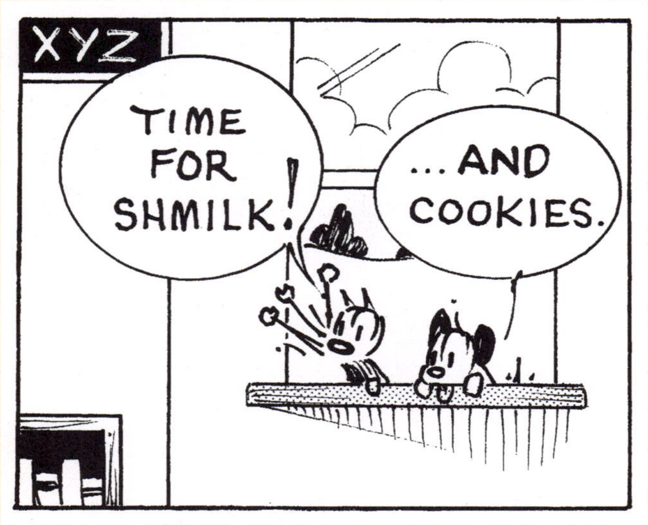
XYZ
TIME FOR SHMILK!
...AND COOKIES.

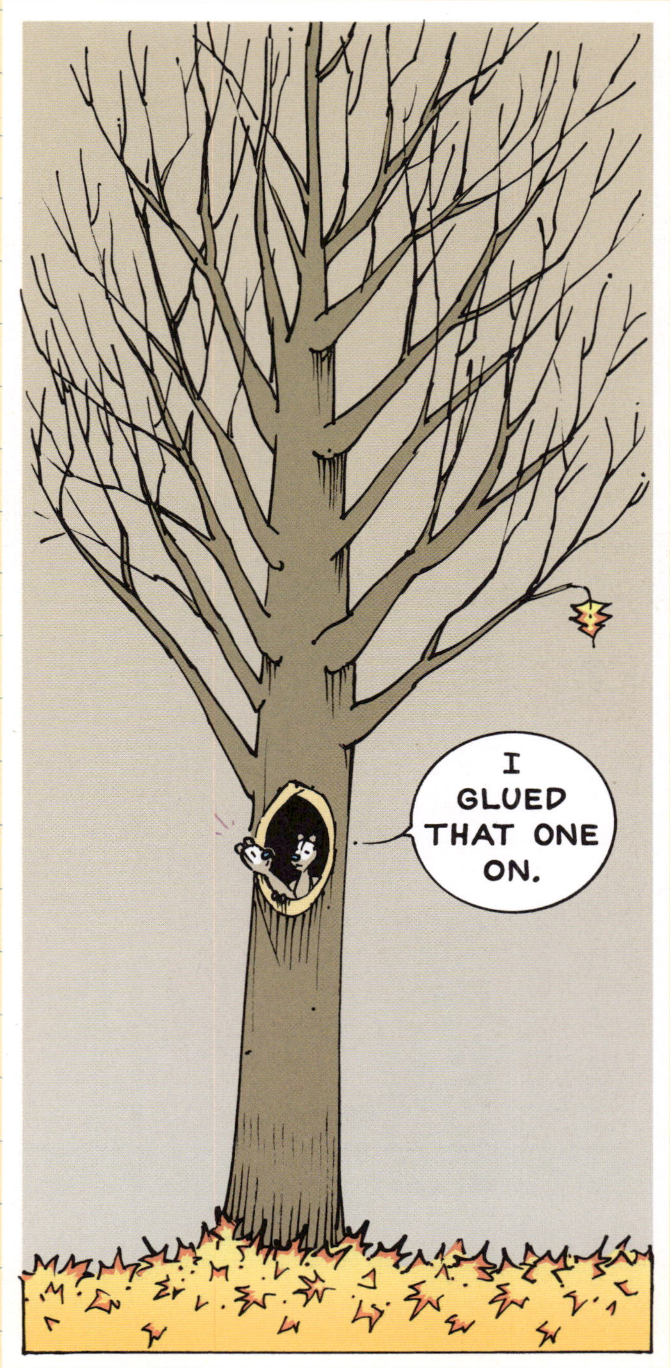
I GLUED THAT ONE ON.

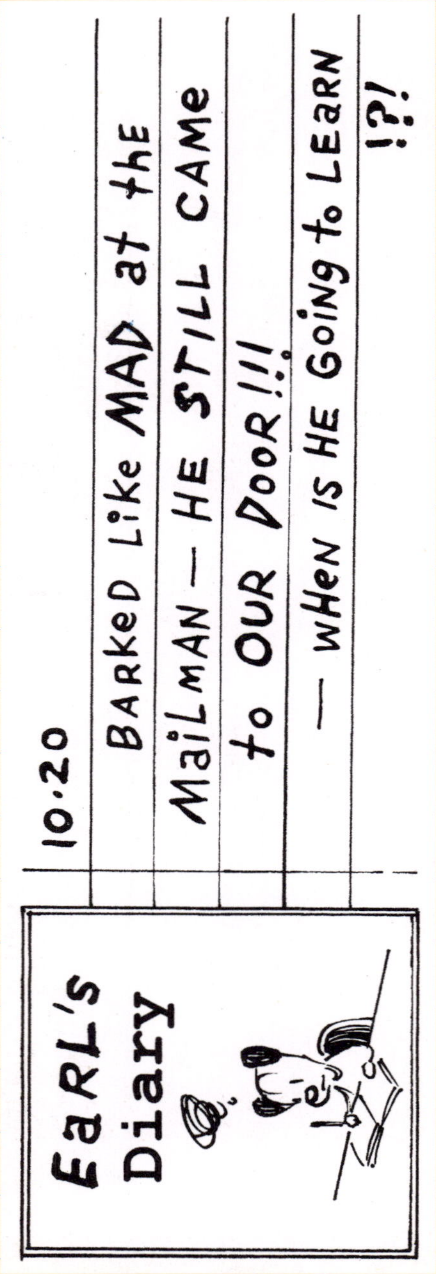
EaRL's Diary
10·20
BARKED Like MAD at the MaiLMAN — HE STILL CAME to OUR DOOR!!!
— wHEN IS HE GOiNg to LEARN !?!

WHAT'S ON THE MENU FOR THANKSGIVING, MILLIE?
BABY CORN, BABY CARROTS, BABY SPINACH, BABY LETTUCE, BABY...
WAH!

EARL-
DINNER!
GOBBLE
GOBBLE
GOBBLE

WHAT'S FOR DESSERT ?

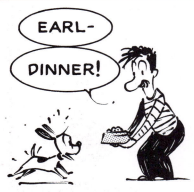

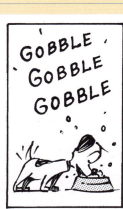

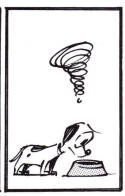

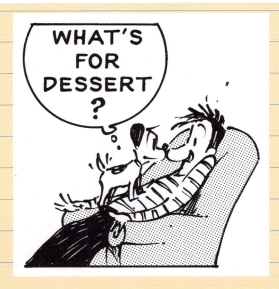

MOOCH!?!

I SHOULDN'T HAVE HAD THAT SECOND PIECE OF PUMPKIN PIE.

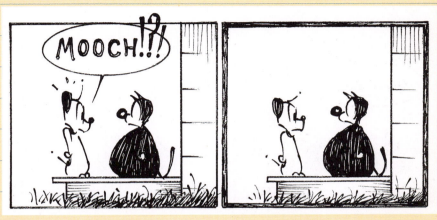

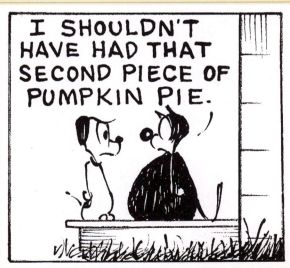

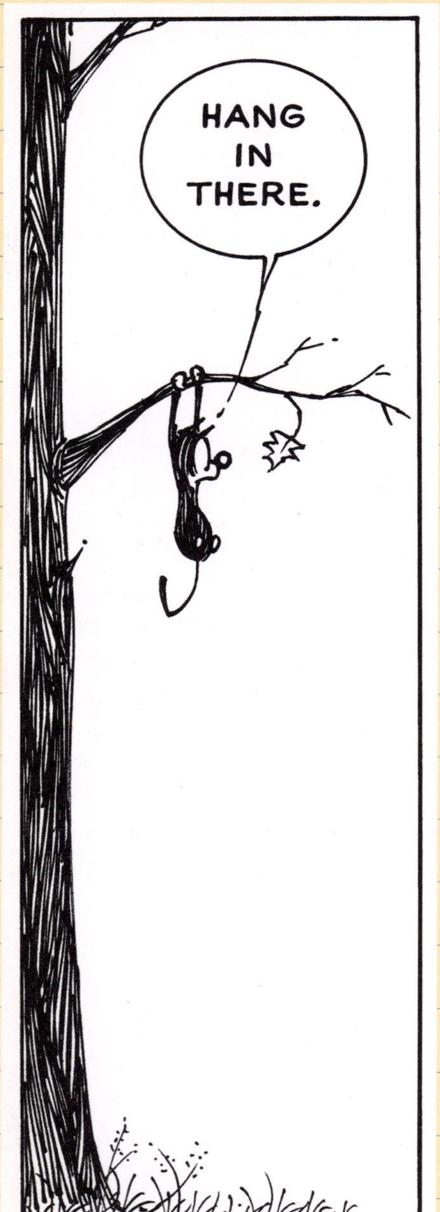
HANG IN THERE.

MORE TO EXPLORE! Learn interesting facts about the animal kingdom!

Q: Can bats walk?

A: Nope! The legs of a bat are so thin that very few species of bat can walk. But who wants to walk when you can soar? Bats are the only mammals that can fly.

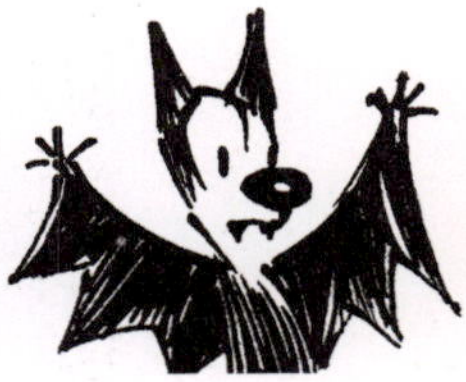

Q: Where are a butterfly's taste buds?

A: On its feet! To determine whether a leaf will make a good spot to lay its eggs, a butterfly will "taste" it by landing on it with its feet.

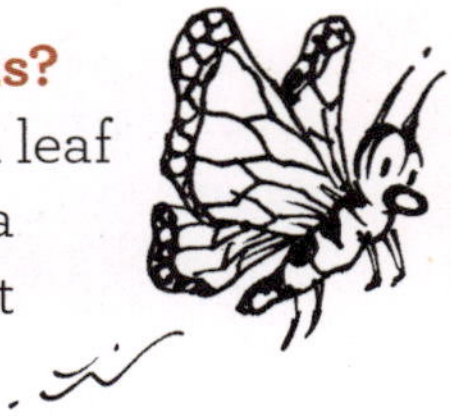

Q: Can squirrels plant trees?

A: Yes! In fact, squirrels plant thousands of trees each year simply by being forgetful. Squirrels often lose track of where they've buried their acorns, and eventually, those forgotten acorns grow into oak trees.

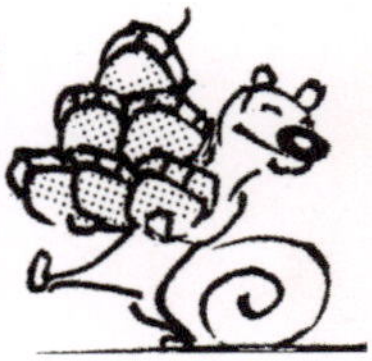

Q: Do frogs drink water?

A: Well, sort of. Frogs drink water by absorbing it through their skin.

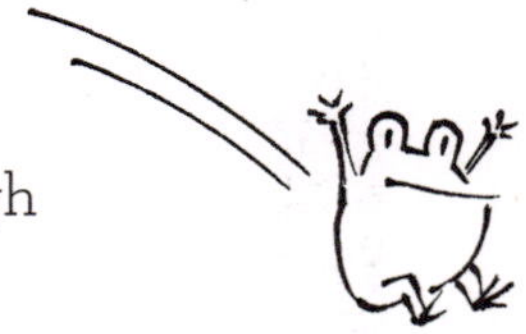

Q: How do you know when a rabbit is happy?

A: Sometimes, when a rabbit is happy, it "binkies," meaning it jumps in the air and twists its body.

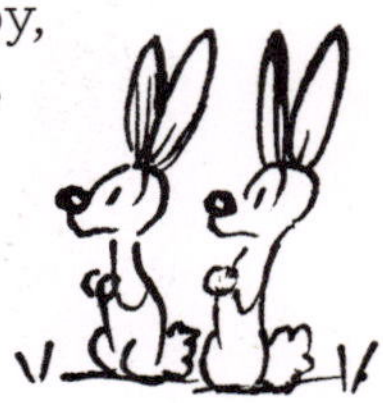

Q: Can tigers swim?

A: Tigers are great swimmers! They can swim up to almost four miles at a time.

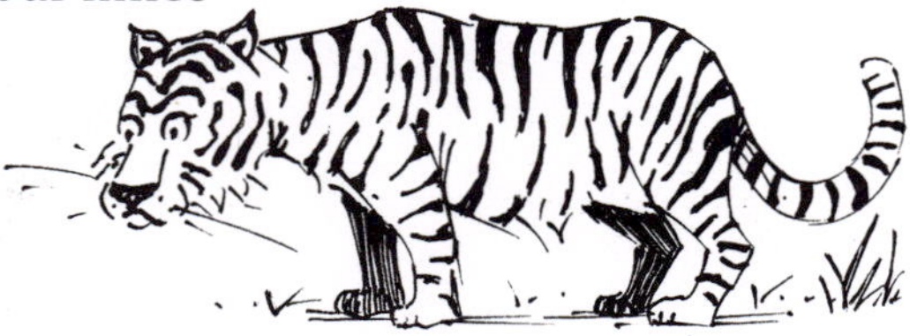

Q: Do whales have teeth?

A: Most whales do not have teeth. Instead, they use a plate of comb-like fiber called baleen to filter their prey from the water.

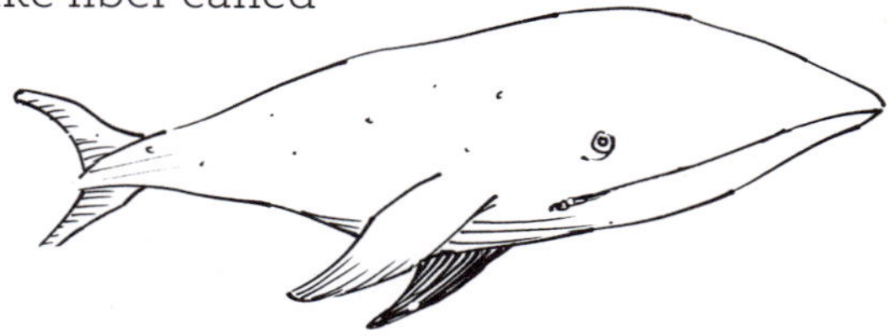

Q: What is an elephant's trunk for?

A: The elephant's trunk has many functions. An elephant uses its trunk to lift food to its mouth, suck water from the ground, and sense the size, shape, and temperature of an object.

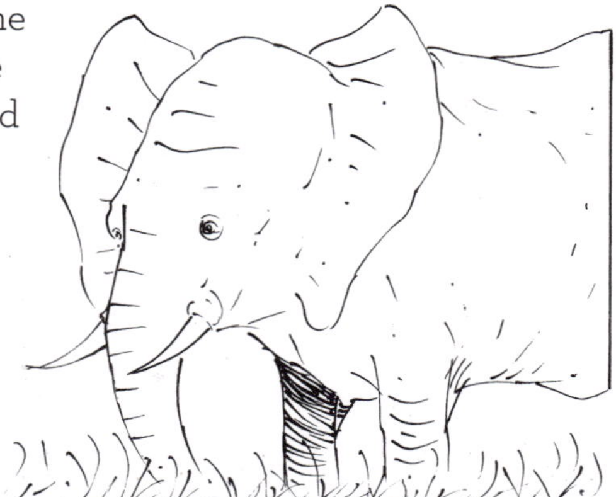

Q: How loud is a lion's roar?
A: Really loud! A lion's roar can be heard up to five miles away.

Q: What do you call a group of dolphins?
A: A school! Dolphins tend to live in schools of up to twelve individuals.

Q: Do leopards live together in groups?
A: Unlike their lion cousins, leopards are solitary animals. Each adult leopard has its own territory and tries to avoid other leopards.

Q: Do moose have antlers year-round?

A: Nope. A male moose only has its antlers from early spring to late autumn. The antlers fall off just before winter. Each spring, a moose grows bigger antlers than it had the previous year!

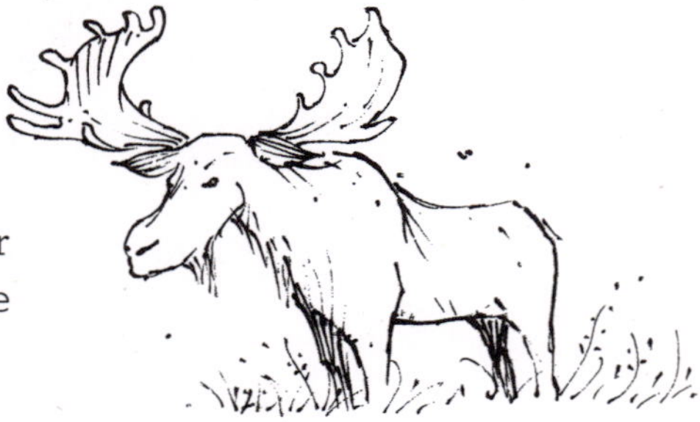

Q: How many hearts does an octopus have?

A: Three!

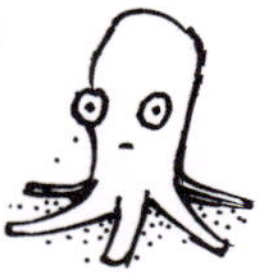

Q: How long have sea turtles existed?

A: Sea turtles are one of the oldest species around. They've been in existence since long before most dinosaurs.

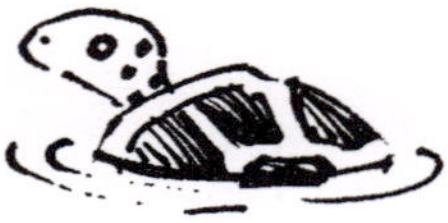

Q: Do hippos use sunblock?

A: Hippos secrete an oily substance from their skin that acts as a sunblock and moisturizer.

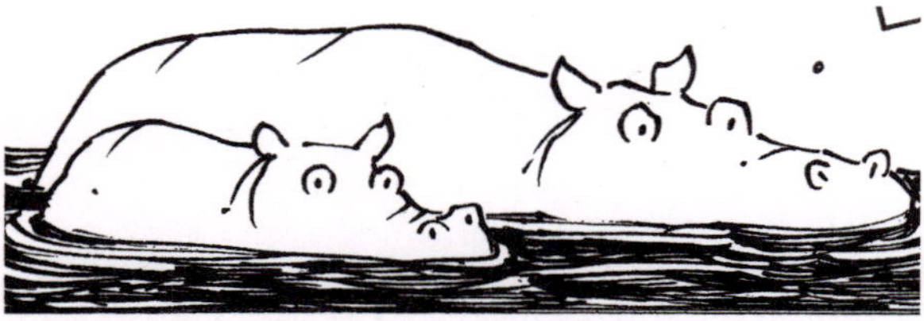

Mutts is distributed internationally by King Features Syndicate, Inc. For information, write to King Features Syndicate, Inc., 300 West Fifty-Seventh Street, New York, New York 10019, or visit www.KingFeatures.com.

Andrews McMeel Publishing
a division of Andrews McMeel Universal
1130 Walnut Street, Kansas City, Missouri 64106

16 17 18 19 20 SDB 10 9 8 7 6 5 4 3 2 1

ISBN: 978-1-4494-8011-0

Library of Congress Control Number: 2016932242

Printed on recycled paper.

Mutts can be found on the Internet at www.mutts.com.

Cover design by Jeff Schulz

Made by:
Shenzhen Donnelley Printing Company Ltd.
Address and location of manufacturer:
No. 47, Wuhe Nan Road, Bantian Ind. Zone,
Shenzhen China, 518129
1st Printing — 7/18/16

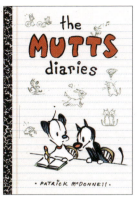
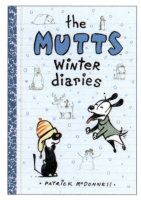
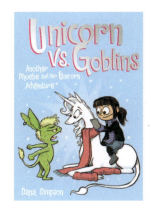
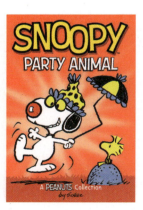
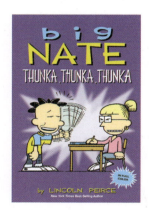
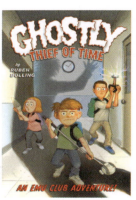
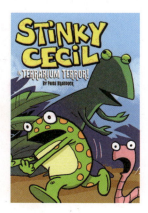
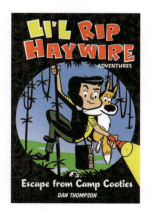
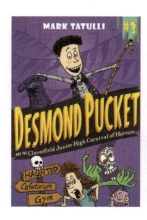